THE HOARSE
OATHS OF FIFE

By the same author:

Trench Fever (Little, Brown, 1998)
Roger, Sausage & Whippet (Headline, 2012)
Greg Dyke – My Part in his Downfall (Universe Press 2015)

THE HOARSE OATHS OF FIFE

Chris Moore

Universe Press

Universe Press
an imprint of Unicorn Publishing Group
66 Charlotte Street
London W1T 4QE

A catalogue record for this book is available from
the British Library

First limited edition

ISBN 978-1-910500-29-3

Cover design by Ryan Gearing
Typeset by Vivian@Bookscribe

Printed and bound in the UK by Berforts, Stevenage

CONTENTS

The Hoarse Oaths of Fife, 1965

The Lost Boys of the Punjab, 1915

... I have perceived much beauty
In the hoarse oaths that kept our
courage straight;
Heard music in the silentness of duty;
Found peace where shell-storms spouted
reddest spate ...

Second-Lieut. Wilfred Owen, Manchester Regiment,
killed in action, 1918. *Apologia pro Poemate Meo.*

THE HOARSE OATHS OF FIFE
OF FIFE
1965

1 SQUADDIES

A diminishing succession of drawers slamming in the room next door suggests that Rasgun might be finishing off whatever it is he's been doing in there for the past half-hour, squeezing into something a little tighter round the hips no doubt. First it was my daughters, then their husbands, now it is their children's turn to take me for granted.

"Are you actually intending to go out like that?"

Rasgun displays a fashionable extent of expensive underpant between the belt of his too-tight hipster jeans and the torn hem of his hooded 'College Boy' sweat-top.

"Won't you find it cold, strutting around with your arse hanging out all night?"

The made-in-Taiwan imitation of a collegiate crest on his chest is quartered as follows: lighted spliff; foaming beer tankard; full ashtray; crossed broken pencils. The parenting books my wife quoted at me all those years ago always stressed the need for honest communication between family members and I've never found that a problem.

"You look like a rent boy."

"Thanks, Grandad, but I really don't have the time for banter."

From me, our daughters inherited a half portion of my pigmentation and weak eyesight. From their mother they received a musical ear and the Welsh instinct for self-interest.

"I need cash," says Rasgun. "And I need it now."

I hold up a twenty pound note worn limp by human contact. "Everything we touch absorbs us, Raz. It's all in the DNA."

He couldn't care less about the gene pool. Every Friday night, in the weeks since Rasgun has been staying in London with us, he has felt the irresistible urge to load his five senses to maximum capacity and party like there's no tomorrow.

"Actually," he says, "it's not a good moment right now – for the DNA and all that – I'm somewhat pressed for time – *and totally fricking skint!*"

Up here at the top of the house it is twenty-seven years since my last daughter flew the nest. Rasgun has moved in with us to help him focus with minimal distraction on re-taking the A-level exams he crashed so spectacularly the first time around. We blame the skunk habit he picked up at that posh boarding school in Scotland his parents sent him to. Despite the attic's wide open sky-light our guest room hums of weed reek. I dispense a crisp new twenty, fresh from the cash-point, un-stained by fingertaint.

"And please, Raz – no phone calls in the middle of the night. As I think I may have told you before, I am not a taxi service."

The drumming of his cowboy boots down three flights of stairs ends with the crash of the front door slamming. Out on the top landing, the trail of his after-shave evaporates slowly. I blame his parents and the distant legacy of the highly conditional love I doled out all those years ago in blatant contravention of the parenting manuals. Next door, in what used to be the girls' shared attic before it became the guest room, I wallow in myself. Half a million family scenes have been played out up here over the decades. I pull books off the shelf. 'Of Mice and Men'. 'To Kill a Mockingbird'. These are the books Megan and Jannat studied for their 'A' levels before bequeathing them to posterity, including those touchstone texts they borrowed from me, such as 'Up the Line to Death – The War Poets, 1914–1918'.

'Gas! Gas! Quick, boys! – An ecstasy of fumbling ...'

Good old Wilfred Owen. Still going strong.

'Above all I am not concerned with Poetry. My subject is War, and the pity of War.'

Jannat's faded popsters scowl down from their 1980s time warp. Megan's furry gonks wait patiently in line. It's never going to happen, guys. They're never coming back. They went to school, they got their grades.

"We're off piddling!"

The front door bangs shut again, drawing me to the window in my study. I watch my wife turn left out of the gate then stand and wait while the dog does his business under the lamp post. Once upon a time, old Rufi used to leap and bark in doggy ecstasy, now he waddles gamely, listing to the right. I check that Rasgun has packed his kit bag like he promised and wander back to my study. I think I'm more excited by our road trip than he is. Tomorrow we'll be heading north for a cricket weekend with his school friends and their folks. Open on my desk is a limp, paper-covered exercise book with a wispy memento adhered to the page – the ghost of a Scottish blossom once pressed for time a lifetime ago. Its tissue petals offer a bleached and scentless testament to the type of teenager I was when I was Rasgun's age.

'Tuesday, 27th June, 1965. Pittendrie Top. 32 acres, Pentland Dell. Sunny with a decent breeze. We didn't disgrace ourselves too much. Blisters. Knackered. Too tired to write.'

* * * * *

They greeted us Fife-style, with shared blank expressions, except for the youngest one who peeped out shyly not knowing what to make of us. They stood apart in the scuffed corner of the Lower Murtry farmyard accorded the roguing squad by custom.

"So," said the gaffer that first morning, "what is it you know about tatties, lads?"

Close up, he smelled sourly of what he'd been drinking the night before. Fredo and I had spent the first two weeks of our university vacation in the potato plots of the local agriculture college. We knew all there was to know about tatties. We were qualified potato roguers with certificates to prove it.

"Well," I announced, "we got Distinctions at Elmfield."

The squad stared in unison at the two freaks in front of them. The fact that Fredo and I had both scored 14 out of 15 on our final Potato Identification and Diseases exam at Elmfield College seemed suddenly to be admirable grounds for reticence.

"Fourteen out o' fifteen?" said the gaffer. "Well fuck me sideways." He stepped forward with his hand out, but not for shaking.

"It's certainly been a while," he said, "since we had that kind o' scholarship around here."

He tested my palm with a calloused thumb. His left eye was cheeky, quizzical, charming, quarrelsome. His right eye was a raptor's eye.

"Anything else you're good at, woggie?" he said. "Apart from the tatties?"

Lichfield Grammar School had taught me plenty about wog, woggie, half-wog, golliwog, Paki-boy, picaninny, half-breed, halfcaste, nig-nog and dirty black bastard.

"Woggie isn't my name," I said. "If you don't mind."

I was also on familiar terms with coon, chocolate-face and Sambo.

"Fair enough," said the gaffer mildly. "No offence intended, you saft, wally English bastard."

He pinched my bicep.

"So where is it you're from then exactly," he said, "down south?"

"Lichfield," I said.

"Lichfield?"

"The heart of England," I said. "I was born in Lahore."

"Ah," said the gaffer. "India. Where the tea comes from. You're an Indi-boy."

"That's right," I said. "Except Lahore's been in Pakistan for quite a while now."

My father was a 'black pot' apothecary in Lahore's British military hospital. He was killed in a car crash before he had time to marry my mum. So strictly speaking, in Kenny's terms, I was indeed a saft, wally bastard. He turned aside.

"And what about you like, good sir? What would your name be?"

"Fredo," said Fredo. "Short for Alfredo."

"Al Fredo," said the gaffer. "That's some kind o' wop name is it not?"

Fredo's dad had arrived from Italy in 1945 with the clothes on his back and a single suitcase. He now owned three chip shops in Streatham, south London. An expensive, sports-orientated education at St. Paul's School had slightly dented Fredo's nose but left intact his immigrant respect for getting ahead. Sport was the thing that had brought the two of us together at St Andrews University, Fife, Scotland, cricket in particular.

"That's right," said Fredo, "a wog and a wop – that's what you've got."

The gaffer pushed his flat cap to the back of his bald spot. The weight of years had given him a slight stoop.

"Hear that lads?" he called. "This is our lucky day. It's a wog and a wop we've got, and English ones at that."

He stroked flat his crest of white hair and appraised us beadily.

"Fuck knows what Davy thinks he's up to with you two," he said, "but we've a heap o' tatties to rogue this year and he says you're the best he could get, so –"

He jerked his thumb over his shoulder.

"So let's be having you."

A battered Bedford van was waiting.

"And your name?" said Fredo. "Kenny," said the gaffer.

"How do you do, Kenny."

Kenny frowned at Fredo's outstretched hand. Around us the farmyard's noise and bustle had risen in volume with the start of the working day. A tanker from the Milk Marketing Board rumbled away with a toot of its horn. There stood Fredo, with his hand out for shaking, and there stood the gaffer not shaking it. Until he did, with a swift motion.

" 'How do you do?' " he said. "We'll see about that."

* * * * *

The dusty back of the Bedford van smelled of petrol and pesticide. The smallest of the three farmboys climbed in the back with us and stretched out on a pile of plastic sacks next to the gaffer's squinting dog. The boy's name was Wee Eck. He had peachy cheeks and hands the size of trowels. The dog's name was Shane. He licked himself and pretended to go to sleep. As the Bedford bumped out of the farm yard I checked the number of fags in my packet of ten Woodbines – seven left – and denied myself. There was no knowing when we might next chance across such a thing as a shop in this part of the world. Kenny halted at a halt sign to let a solitary, early car bumble by.

"Come on, Missus," he muttered, "hurry yourself. We're on a fucking job o' work here, if you don't mind."

He turned right and banked the van uphill. Those of us in the back slid about in a cloud of chaff. Empty bottles of fizzy pop rattled against the rear doors. Then we jolted off-road.

"Shift it, lads," said Kenny. "Hoist your hipes."

The two farmboys who'd taken the Bedford's front seat climbed out and stretched themselves yawningly. The freckled one with the red hair went over to the barbed wire fence and peed on it. His name was Tamas. His big, lumpy colleague, Bender, found a space of his own and stood in it, as if to scent the air. Fredo and I nervously assessed our first real potato crop. The days of theory were behind us. Kenny fixed me with his eagle eye.

"So. What have we got here, College Boy? What kind o' crop are we looking at here?"

I examined closely the tatties in question, the shape of their leaves, their colour and texture. Crop identification was the beginning and end of the potato roguer's craft. Was there a pattern in the grouping of leaflets on their stems? Any tint of colouration? It was too early in the season for any flower buds to have opened so there were no clues there. My head had drained of everything I'd learned in the seed plots of Elmfield College.

"Pentland Dell?" I ventured.

Guessing was the best I could do. With their big yield and alleged higher tolerance to disease, the Pentland family was taking the Scottish potato scene by storm.

"Dell?" said Kenny. "Pentland Dell? Anyone else got any bright ideas?"

Bender was immersed in the hedge, choosing himself a branch to snap off to make a roguing stick. Tamas, having finished irrigating the fence, was bent over the van's wing mirror tending his coiffure. At Kenny's call, he gave a final slick to his quiff and holstered his comb in the back pocket of his jeans.

"I'm so damned good-looking," he declared, "if I was a lassie I'd have to shunt myself."

Kenny pointed with his stick.

"College Boy reckons it's a crop o' Dell, Tamas."

Tamas swaggered past with an air of expert condescension.

"Dell?" he sneered. "If that's no a field o' Pentland Crown then our college chum here's the Milky Bar Kid."

The farmboys laughed obediently. I had been dealing with Tamases all my life. No offence intended, Gunga Din.

"Bender?" said Kenny.

Bender was built like a bear – a bear with a bad complexion.

"Aye," he grumped, scratching the divot of yellowish thatch on top of his head. "Or could it be a crop o' that new Dutch stuff, Kenny? Eh?"

The gaffer refused to be drawn.

"Wee Eck?" he said.

"It's looking like Crown to me right enough," said the peachy one, pronouncing it Fife-style, the same as the others – *Croon*.

"And you like," said Kenny, "Signor Tinkerbello-what's-your-name-again?"

"Fredo," said Fredo. "Short for Alfredo. You do have a short memory, Kenny. Yes. It does look rather Crown-like."

"Crown?" said Kenny. "So that's what you all think. Thirty acres o' Pentland Crown is it?"

He puffed out his chest.

"Well all I can say is, if that's the best you can do this squad is fucked before we've even started. I mean, for fucksake, lads – when did you ever see a field o' Crown looking this well grown in June? Eh? Of course it's fucking Dell. Well done, College."

"Could be that them Distinctions o' theirs might come in handy after all, Kenny," said Bender judiciously.

I stood there modestly, astounded and grateful.

"Come on," said Kenny, turning on his heel. "Stop blethering all day like a bunch o' women and fall in."

The farmboys pulled dusty plastic sacks from the back of the van and began tying them round their legs with frayed twists of orange baler twine. Fredo tucked his brand new jeans into the top of his new wellies and I did the same. We couldn't see the point of the plastic sacks and were too proud to ask. The five of us shuffled into line. Kenny faced us and straightened his left shoulder. Above his old boots he had swaddled his legs in puttee-style gaiters improvised from strips of torn plastic.

"Right," he announced. "It's the first day o' this year's season so it's welcome to the squad, you new boys, and listen up. Two drills apiece is the name o' the game until we get our eye in. That's one drill apiece each side. If you see anything suspicious in your drill, you call us all over for a look-see. There's no rush today. It takes a while to get your eye in at the start o' the season. Remember, you can't rogue it if you can't see it and you can't see it if you don't know what you're looking for. Understood?"

No one spoke.

"Right, then. College and Fredo, you stick with me in the middle so I can keep an eye on you. Tamas and Bender, you're the flankers. Wee Eck, you're the scout, out wide. Ready, lads? Then let's away –"

We entered the crop in squad order with a single ploughed drill planted with potatoes on each side of us. Fredo and I lagged half a stride behind so we could copy the others' moves without making it obvious. They headed for the far end of the field, searching the plants to left and right, stopping now and then to prod one with a stick for the benefit of closer inspection. We were looking for rogues – any potato plants in the crop that were not Pentland Dells. We were also searching for any evidence of disease of sickness. Suddenly, Fredo and I were proper roguers. Our job for the next six weeks was to walk up and down drilled fields of potatoes all day, hauling out rogues and sickies and putting them in the sacks on our backs. We soon realised why the farmboys had wrapped their legs in plastic. Within minutes our jeans were soaked through with dew from the sodden plants that reached up to our knees. At the top of the field we emerged from our drills and emptied our sacks in a heap.

"Call that tattie roguing?" said Kenny.

He picked through the pile of dumped plants with the sceptical point of his stick. Discarded potato specimens were known in the trade as shaws. Between us we had found no rogues and only a few sickies, mainly leaf-rolls.

"If you call that tattie roguing," said Kenny, spearing a particular shaw with his stick and shaking it in the air, "what in the holy name o' fuck do you call this cheeky wee bastard?"

Pale, immature potato nodules bobbled on their hairy rootlets.

"Well?" he demanded.

Tamas picked off a white node and crunched it between his teeth.

"Fucked if I know," he said. "Tastes like shite, though."

"Bender?"

Bender snapped off a sprig of leaves to take back to the crop for the purpose of close comparison. They looked no different from all the others.

"Jesus Christ and God Almighty," sighed Kenny. "And here was me thinking you was tattie roguers. It's a *Pentland Crown*, for fucksake."

My earlier triumph of identification meant nothing more than beginner's luck. If spotting the difference between a Pentland Crown and a Pentland Dell was the mark of a proper roguer on the first day of the season Fredo and I were, indeed, fucked. In genetic terms, Pentland Crown and Pentland Dell were siblings. In practical terms, Fredo and I didn't have a clue. Kenny tossed the offending Crown aside.

"And who's drill do you think I found that in?" he said

Fredo and I looked at the wellies on our feet. They were green and new to the game, like us.

"In your drill, College."

I felt myself blushing and hated myself. Me and my Distinctions. I prodded my specs back to the top of my nose and said nothing.

"Lesson number one," said Kenny, "nobody takes nothing for granted in this squad. *Comprenny-voo*? Canny is the way we do it, Fife-style. And the first one to get me another Crown in this crop gets a florin for it."

Every crop of potatoes was a battle to Kenny. His sworn enemies were the inspectors from the Ministry of Agriculture who were tasked each year with grading the health of the Scottish potato crop. Every field of seed potatoes in the country had to be checked. Certificates of quality were only granted to those crops that could be shown, on the basis of a statistically valid sample, to be free of rogues or sickies. Leaf-roll was the most common disease. It caused the potato plant to curl up and turn yellow. Blackleg was less serious but more common, a bacterial infection that caused the entire plant to rot from within and collapse. Mild mosaic was also a threat, a virus spread by insects and chiefly identifiable by a light mottling of the leaves.

As roguers, our job was to weed each field until it was clean for inspection. 'FS1' was the highest grade of certificate; 'AAA' was the lowest. The higher the grade, the higher the price the crop would fetch. Failure was not an option at Lower Murtry. Fredo and I had joined an elite and Kenny wanted to keep it that way. Only later, days later, did he confess that the rogue Pentland Crown he found in my drill was, in fact, a perfectly healthy Pentland Dell. The whole thing was a stunt to get us on our mettle early on. No one got the florin off Kenny that day, nor the next.

"Sharp eyes and plenty o' *jildi*," said Kenny. "That's what you need for roguing."

"*Jildi*?"

In Kenny's old army lingo, *jildi* meant energy, hard work or, as an injunction, shift it.

"I would've thought you'd have known about *jildi*, young College" he said, "being as how it's a woggie word and all. We picked up all kinds o' lingo in the army. *Blighty* … *bint* …."

"I told you," I said. "I'm not a *pukka* woggie. I'm English."

"Well, half of you is," said Kenny, "and that's caution enough to be going on with."

2 SUMMER HOUSE

Those first days at Pittendrie Top set the pattern for Lower Murtry's 1965 potato roguing season. We rogued hard each morning and stopped for our pieces when the sun reached its height. Kenny had first choice of the coolest spot, then the farmboys chose theirs. Fredo and I were welcome to whatever bit of midday shade might be left over.

"So, you saft, wally English bastards," said Bender, "what pieces has she given you today?"

Piece was the Fife word for a sandwich. Bender poked his snout into the Tupperware box of pieces made up for us by Wilma, the Lower Murtry housekeeper. The farmer, Davy Morrison, was deducting five shillings a day from our wages for board and lodging.

"Fucking poofy the way she cuts them crusts off for you," said Bender.

His own piece was the heel of a loaf folded round a wedge of sweaty cheese, followed by two packets of crisps and two Mars bars.

"That's because bread crusts is against the Hindoo religion," said Tamas.

"Is that no right, College?"

I continued tending the blister on my foot.

"I've told you already, Tamas, I am not a Hindu."

"Hindoo or heathen," he said, "if your Pa was a Paki you'll be one or the other."

"My father was a Muslim."

"Was?" said Bender.

"He died," I said. "He was a Muslim not a Hindu."

My father died after my mother got pregnant but before they could get married. So I was indeed, from Tamas' point of view, a Paki-faced English bastard.

"And what exactly is a Muslim," said Bender, "when he's at home?"

"I'll tell you what your Muzzie-boy is," said Kenny. "He's a fighter, that's what he is."

So far, Kenny had been following the conversation with sardonic indifference. Now he brought the full weight of his accumulated wisdom to bear.

"See, your Muzzie-boy, Ben, he's bred to the warrior code. Stay well out o' the way when *he* gets into his rage o' righteousness. I know what I'm talking about. We had Muzzies alongside us in the war and by Christ they did their bit."

"Wheesht!" said Tamas. "You and your war."

"As a matter of fact," said Fredo, "Islam means peace and a Muslim, Bender, is a follower of Islam, so –"

So suddenly I was surrounded by experts.

"I thought you were a Roman Catholic?" I said.

"Aw, Christ!" said Bender. "That's all we need. First off, our woggie here's a Muzzie-boy. Next thing is, our wop's a left-footer!"

"All wops are left-footers," said Fredo. "It's compulsory."

"And I've told you already, I am not a Muzzie-boy."

"You must be something," said Bender. "Everyone's got to be something."

"I am something," I said. "I'm English."

"That's not a religion," said Tamas, "that's a curse. Religion is what you believe in. And anyway, you're only half English so that means we've got the worst of both ends."

"Wheesht with your blethers," said Kenny. "Strong drink and dominoes, lads – that's the creed for the working man. God's just a matter of opinion when it comes to religion. Now then, who's got the fags? Seems like I've left mine in the van again."

I passed round my packet of Woodbines and we puffed in silence for a while. When Bender discarded his 'Daily Record' I pounced on it for news of the English County Championship. The last news I'd heard was that Worcestershire were losing touch with the leaders.

"Cricket?" sneered Tamas. "Is that no some kind o' game for English poofs?"

The Sports pages of the 'Daily Record' were entirely silent on the subject.

"You're right there, Tamas," said Bender. "Cricket's the game for poofs alright. Fucking white trousers. The hammer, College, that's the real game, throwing the hammer."

"In England," I said, "throwing the hammer's the game for poofs who can't play cricket."

"Aye," said Fredo. "He's no wrong there, lads. It's muckle popular wi' the poofiest poofs down south, is yon fucking hammer-throwing, ya cunt ye."

Kenny's laughter ended with the coughing-up of matter and its noisy expulsion.

"Finish your blethers, you lads," he wheezed, "and let's get this field done and dusted. Then we can go home early again."

Wee Eck handed over a stick he'd been whittling for me.

"Thanks," I said. "I've been looking for a good one."

I weighed my new roguing stick in each hand to get the feel of it. I tried a few cricket shots and took guard in front of an imaginary wicket. When Fredo lobbed me a potato tuber I smashed it to smithereens. It was a great stick, if a trifle sticky round the gripping end. Wee Eck showed me his clasp knife.

"You can borrow this anytime you want, College," he said. "It comes in handy for whittling and stuff like that."

Handsome Fredo, with his height advantage and his assured manner, had been accepted as himself. I, with my woggie skin and National Health spectacles, had become 'College'. It could have been so much worse. I bowled a tuber at Fredo and he whacked it with his stick. Then Kenny took a shy at him, whipping his tuber in low and hard.

"Here, you two," he said, scraping a line in the dirt with the heel of his boot.

He gathered up three ball-sized tatties from the dump of shaws in the endrig.

"Let's see how good you cricketers really are. Best o' three gets the winnings."

Kenny's target was the roof of the Bedford van, parked by the gate about thirty yards away. The prize, again, was his un-winnable florin. He beckoned Fredo to the mark.

"Ladies first –"

The farmboys jeered from the sidelines as Fredo's first effort span wide while Kenny's spud landed plumb on target. Kenny kept his arm straight for throwing, like a bowler. The Bedford's tin roof sent out a hollow bang. My own straight-armed lob missed by a bare yard. "Scotland the Brave – one," called out Tamas, "poofy English bastards – nil."

Bang! Kenny's second tattie landed as cleanly as the first, right on the Bedford's roof. When I missed again, the hammer throwers crowed delightedly. But by this stage we had all got our eye in and all three of us scored with our final shots. Scotland the Brave – three, Useless English Cunts – two. Kenny span his two bob bit and pocketed it for another day.

"Aye," he said, "you English got your eye in too late, as usual. That was the whole story o' the fucking war for us, that was."

Under his eagle eye we lined up in squad order to face the afternoon's job of work.

"Kenny," I said, "where did you learn to bowl like that?"

In we plunged, into the first yards of Pittendrie's long, steep, ankle wrenching drills of potatoes.

"A chap called Sergeant Sullivan trained me," said Kenny. "At the bombing school."

He paused in his drill alongside me.

"He was the best bomber in the British Army, Sergeant Sullivan, and it wasn't just bombs he taught us neither."

Bombs, to my mind, were big, heavy things dropped from planes. Kenny was talking about hand grenades.

"They were bringing out new bombs every day o' the week after Neuve Chapelle," he said. "They thought bombs were going to win the war for us."

"Which war was that?"

Kenny's eagle eye blazed indignantly.

" 'Which war was that?' " he squawked. "Christ lad, the Great War! Which fucking war did you think I was fucking talking about? The First World War, College, the Great War for Civilization, 1914 – 1918."

Ahead of us, the squad trudged into the distance, wading through the knee-high potato crop with gaps in the line where Kenny and I were absent.

" 'What passing bells,' " I said, " 'for those who die as cattle? Only the monstrous anger of the guns.' "

It bubbled up from somewhere I couldn't quite remember.

"Aye," said Kenny, " 'monstrous anger' sounds about right. That was the Great War alright. Monstrous. Now let's be putting some *jildi* into it, for fucksake, or we'll never catch up."

* * * * *

When we got back to Lower Murtry Kenny parked the van in its vault in the old, stone-built steading and disappeared without ceremony. Everyone in the squad had somewhere to go except me and Fredo. Davy Morrison was nowhere to be seen. Wilma, the wasp-waisted housekeeper, was busy in the kitchen of the big house with her back to the open door.

"That smells good," said Fredo, meaning the dinner..

"Aye," she said. "Then mind you're back for it at five o'clock."

Fredo tendered his empty Tupperware box. Wilma carried on peeling potatoes at the sink.

"And for the last time of asking," she said, "filthy wellies are not allowed inside the house. Take them off at the door if you must come charging in here like a couple o' mucky bullocks."

Wilma's way of looking sideways was as sharp as flint. It was difficult to imagine any man getting the better of her. Lower Murtry's big house was her absolute domain.

"You'll not see Davy afore dinner," she said. "He's off somewhere with a load o' berries. And shut the door on your way out."

We found some shade in the yard and watched the dairyman, Wee Eck's dad, using a whittled stick to get his ladies into line for the evening yield. A tractor bustled round the corner and headed for the berry field with a trailer loaded with plastic barrels bouncing behind it. Lower Murtry Farm was all about work; with none of our own to do Fredo and I were superfluous.

The stepped terrace at the back of the big house led down to what had once been a tennis court or croquet lawn. In the corner, behind the hanging boughs of a fine beech, lurked an old summer house with a cutely skewed stove-pipe chimney. It had two rooms inside.

"Someone's been in here," said Fredo, picking up the stub of a candle.

We kicked off our green wellies and shook out the mulch of soggy potato leaves that had gathered inside each one. Fredo arranged a dusty cushion and stretched his long bones.

"Five weeks to go," he sighed. "Reckon we'll make it?"

The wooden joists of the summer house settled and creaked. We had to make it. How else were we going to pay for our Inter-Rail odyssey round the capitals of Europe? I gave Fredo a Woodbine and lit one for myself. Outside, the farm's portable sawmill whined for one last time and fell silent. Swollen cows butted against their stalls in the milking parlour. At a quarter past five we heard the scrunch of tyres on gravel and disposed of our cigarette butts through a crack in the floorboards.

"So," said Davy Morrison, when we entered the kitchen, "what was it like today, lads?"

Davy Morrison was a blond beast with soft, grey eyes. He stood at the head of the table, scooping hot potatoes from the dish with dirty hands. Wilma had set the scene as pretty as a picture, with a jug of garden flowers in the centre.

"I'm away then, Davy," she chirruped. "I'll see thee the morn's morn."

Wilma folded her last tea towel and threaded it through the handle of the oven door and reached both hands behind to undo the knot of her apron strings. Nothing was too good for Davy. He grunted by way of acknowledgement.

"Where did Kenny take you today, lads?" he said, cramming in another mouthful.

The Morrison family silver gleamed.

"Pittendrie again."

"Oh aye?" said Davy. "And does Hector's stuff look clean enough for us?"

Dribs and drabs of strawberry juice had dried in the shape of tattoos on his hairy forearms.

"Oh aye," said Fredo, passing me the serving spoon. "Just a wee bit o' blackleg. And a touch o' leaf-roll here and there."

"And was Kenny alright with you?" said Davy.

"Oh aye," I said. "He was fine, like."

"Bender?"

"He was fine too."

"If that boy challenges you to any arm-wrestling while you're here," said Davy, "say no. Ben doesn't like the English as a rule."

"Thanks," I said. "We're getting used to that."

Davy wiped his hands on the back of his shorts and delved into another bowl piled with his own strawberries. There were six chairs round the table, only three places set. Beyond Wilma's kitchen, the rest of the Murtry big house exuded a tidy, intimidating atmosphere. There was no evidence of a wife, children or pets, just the right amount of space to accommodate them one day when the right woman and her dowry came along.

"Help yourself to what you fancy," said Davy, wiping his hands again and moving off, "and stick the dishes in the sink when you're finished. There's a brand new telly next door if you're in the mood."

No telly for him. Hard work from dawn to dusk was all the entertainment any Morrison needed.

"A wee bit on the gruff side, aren't they?" said Fredo.

"Aye," I said, "just a wee bit gruffy. Now shut yer puss an' finish yer fucking dinner, ya saft wally English bastard ye."

3 PITTENDRIE TOP

On our last day at Pittendrie Top farm, Kenny added an extra half hour to the piece break because it was so hot. Also, Hector Morrison's fields were so clean there could be no doubt they were heading straight for an FS1 grade. We lazed at ease with the Firth of Tay spread out below. Eastward, the estuary widened and vanished into the North Sea's ambient blue haze. On the far northern shore, the square tower of Errol's old kirk dominated the patchwork of farms like the last rook on a chess board.

"So what's it like, Fredo," yawned Bender, "that you're studying at yon Uni?"

Bender was greedy by nature and a bit of a bully. On the plus side, he was an honest worker and big enough to keep a check on Tamas' more spiteful inclinations.

"I'm doing pre-Med," said Fredo between chews on his piece.

"Anatomy. Biology. Physiology. Zoology."

The dog Shane drooled with his head on Fredo's knee.

"Are you going to be sensible, College," said Bender, "and leave that ham and cheese one for me to finish off for you?"

I handed Bender one of Wilma's trimmed pieces. Lower Murtry was the centre of Bender's universe. He had been born on the farm. Tamas, by comparison, was a rover. His family now lived at Gunnie, fourteen miles away in the direction of Auchterader where life as an apprentice telephone engineer was already beginning to chafe his aspirations. Tamas was engaged to a Gunnie girl called Muriel, known to the rest of the squad as the Princess. That's why he was working on the farm instead of taking a summer holiday from the GPO. As soon as Tamas and the Princess could afford to get hitched they were emigrating to Australia on an assisted passage.

"And what about you?" said Bender. "What is it you're studying yourself, young College?"

"Eng. Lang. and Lit. – English Language and Literature."

Bender and Tamas choked theatrically in feigned outrage. Fredo's doctoring they could understand but –

"Hear that, Kenny?" said Bender. "The English are sending their woggies up to St Andrews to learn their own fucking language!"

"I'll bet it's yon Shakespeare he's conning up," said Kenny. "The English are right keen on their bard."

"We did one o' Shakey's pomes once in Miss Mawhinney's class," said Bender. "Fucked if I can remember a word o' it."

" 'Friends, Romans, countrymen,' " quoted Tamas, " 'lend us your pricks.' "

English was only part of my Matriculation course at St Andrews. I was also doing Philosophy (compulsory) and Fine Art (optional).

"Great stuff," said Tamas. "That sounds like a real bargain for Scotland – teaching English wogs about pomes and fucking picters while the rest o' us slave our guts out paying income tax at five and six in the pound. It's Oz for me, lads. Australia. And you too, Ben, if you've got any sense."

Bender helped himself to the last piece in my sandwich box.

"Pomes and picters?" he said. "Christ, College, where's the use in them?"

"It'll be the Auld Maisters, Ben," explained Kenny, "the ancient wisdom. There's a whole heap o' savvy out there and some clever cunt's got to con it up for us. If College here wants to gawp at picters all day long and swot up his Eng. Lit. that's fine by me. Especially as he's so generous with his smokes."

I passed round the new packet of Embassy Regal I'd bought at Crean Post Office. If a serious cigarette was needed Kenny would roll his own, out of his brass tin of makings. Otherwise, he was willing to sample anything on offer and Embassy Regals were Scotland's most *pukka* fags. My matches had got squashed in my back pocket and gave trouble lighting.

"Aye," said Kenny, cupping the flame, "I mind at Loos, College, the gas got in our fags so bad you couldn't light the bloody things neither. Awful it was, the Battle o' Loos."

"Aw Christ," groaned Tamas. "I hope this is no another one o' your fucking war stories, you blethering old bletherer?"

"If this is the one," said Bender, "where you catch the German bomb and chuck it back I can probably tell it better than you can yourself, Kenny, I've heard it so often."

Kenny exhaled a thin stream of smoke on the end of his fag to make it glow.

"Like I was saying, College, afore I was so rudely interrupted, there we all were at the Battle o' Loos, September 25th, 1915, me and the lads down in this here fucking Johnson hole wi' old Jerry battering away at us full pelt on his mangle, nothing to eat, nothing to drink and the only fucking fags we had was all minging with gas and totally fucking toxic. So you can imagine the state we were in. No sign o' the rest of the mob, no reinforcements, no officers, no orders, no nothing."

"You should have sent for the cavalry," suggested Tamas. "That's what they do on the telly."

"So," said Kenny. "So we says to Pal Duncan, 'Pally, my son, sneak out the back way and see what's what.' Christ, we was parched. Those fucking gas hoods they put us in were hellish for working up a thirst. You couldn't breathe in them. So Pally sneaks out the back o' the hole and snaggles around for a while on his belly and fuck me sideways if he doesn't find a water bottle on a dead officer with both his legs blown off and a silver fag case in his pocket."

Kenny drew deep on his Regal.

"But see that fucking gas," he continued, "it had taken all the silver off that fag case and turned it greenish-looking. But the fags inside were fine because o' the cork seal. Except they were fucking Turkish weren't they, and that was the first time any o' us had ever seen a Turkish fag, never mind smoked one. But we was ganting, like I says, so we decided to take our chances. And by Christ they were fucking shite. Black as tar, they were. They reeked, sir, they totally fucking reeked. Un-fucking-smoke-able by any definition. Our Billy took one drag on his Turkish fag and he coughed it straight out. 'No offence, old son,' he says to Pally, 'but you can keep the fucking things yourself, I'll take my chances wi' the gas.' Eh, boys!? *Fucking take my chances wi' the gas!* Jesus wept but it's true enough, that story – I was there!" Kenny's cackle of laughter turned into a coughing fit.

"And the thing is," he gasped, "that was our own fucking gas that smothered us at Loos so where's the logic in that, Mr Philosopher?

And it's still in me. It'll kill me for sure one o' these days, Old Jerry's gas."

Kenny coughed his last and spat the final product into the hedge. In those days, Philosophy for first year students in the Arts Faculty of St Andrews University meant Plato's theory of forms, a bit of Descartes and a few chapters of logic, courtesy of Bertrand Russell.

"Have you ever heard of the syllogism?" I said.

"You what?"

"It's the basic form of deductive reasoning – from premises to conclusions. All potatoes are plants; all plants need sun and water; therefore all potatoes need sun and water."

"Oh, that's fucking brilliant that is," said Tamas. "Remind me to get myself a university education one o' these days, Kenny, when I've nothing better to do than sit around all day talking gobshite. 'All tatties are plants.' That's a fine piece o' fucking reasoning that is. 'All tatties need sun and water.' Christ, we don't need no black bastard o' an English woggie to teach us that, for fucksake."

"Don't mind him, College," said Kenny. "Tamas here's a confirmed ignoramus. You carry on, son. Give us another one o' your silly 'jisms till we get the hang o' it."

"All men are human beings," I said. "All women are human beings. Therefore all men are women."

"You what!?"

"How's that, for fucksake?"

"It's a fallacy," I said. "It's a bad argument."

"You're fucking right it's a bad argument," confirmed Bender. "It's a fucking hopeless argument. In fact, it isn't one."

"Is it true that all men are human beings?"

"Aye."

"Is it true that all women are human beings?"

"Aye."

"So why is it false that all men are women?"

"Take a look between your legs," said Bender, "and you'll find the red end o' your plonker staring you right in the face. Facts is facts, College, and there's an end o' it."

"If your end is red, Bender," said Fredo, "I'd take it to the doctor if I was you."

"Logic," I said, "has got fuck all to do with the facts, Ben. The *facts* may be right but the *argument* can still be wrong. In this case, it's because of what logicians call the fallacy of the undistributed middle."

When Kenny and the boys said 'fuck all' it sounded fine. When I said it Fredo cringed with embarrassment on my behalf.

"Is this gobshite I'm hearing," said Tamas, "or is it complete and utter gobshite?"

"All I'm saying," I said, "is that you can have true premises and false conclusions if you don't argue properly – and that's Logic."

"Well if that's the case," said Bender, "Tamas here is right. Logic's just another fancy word for gobshite."

"Aye," said Tamas. "Fallacy o' the fancy fucking fanny-hole is what I calls it, Ben."

He sucked the last of the taste from his apple core and aimed it at Wee Eck's head and Shane chased after it and gobbled it up. Wee Eck just smiled like the champion listener he was and carried on whittling. The only personal data I'd been able to wheedle out of Wee Eck was that he kept a hedgehog in his shed and was a keen collector of bird's eggs. He rose with smiling dignity and carefully folded his blade.

"Time for our off, I reckon," he said.

"Christ, I'm fading fast," wheezed Kenny, hauling himself up on Wee Eck's helping hand. "My symptoms are definitely playing up today, lads. Must be all that talk o' the gas. Fuck knows how much I swallowed out there. What do you recommend, Doctor Fredo, for a double dose o' Jerry's phosgene?"

"Whisky and fags," said Fredo. "Lots of both. At frequent, regular intervals."

"Well off you go to the van and get me some, Wee Eck," said Kenny, "or I'll soon be a goner."

"Sooner the better," said Tamas.

Wee Eck came back from the van with the bottle that Kenny stored among his greasy rags and spanners under the dashboard. Battle juice he called it – a mixture of cold tea and whatever inspiriting liquor he could afford, rum for preference but more usually whisky. It was the only medicine Kenny believed in.

"Now get up, you lazy wee shites. *Raus* it, for fucksake."

"It's too hot," said Fredo. "Trust me. I know what I'm talking about. We'll all get sunstroke or dehydration."

We each clung stubbornly to our last moments in the shade. The red poppies and white trumpets of Briony drowsed on in the long grass under the hedge.

"Relax, Kenny," said Tamas. "This lot's all the same planting so we're home and dry."

What he meant was that because Davy's brother, Hector Morrison, had planted the same prime seed in every one of his fields at Pittendrie our last crop of Dell was guaranteed to be as healthy as the first.

"These cunts are so clean," confirmed Bender, "they could rogue themselves."

"Get thee behind me, Satan," said Kenny. "There'll be no skimping at the roguing while I'm in charge. Give this last crop a good going over, boys, and we'll be home again by four."

Nobody moved. A bumble-bee buzzed among the poppies. The midday torpor had entered us like a drug, dissolving the will to work. Kenny switched from a coaxing tone to a rasp.

"*Raus* it, you skiving bastards. *Ally veet*! That's French. It means shift your bastard arses. Come on, shift it. *Jildi, jildi*."

Fredo got up first and hauled me after him. Bender reluctantly followed our example, then Tamas. Impressed behind us in the long grass we left the six forme-like shapes that made us a squad. Zombie-like we faced up to Pittendrie's tapering drills and trudged into action. Kenny drew alongside, matching me step for step.

"I can see we're in for some fine discourse this season, College," he said cheerfully, the battle-juice having had its tonic effect. "*Cogito ergo sum*. That's the name o' the game."

From what I had been able to deduce, tractors, cars, guns, motorbikes and fishing had previously supplied the Murtry roguing squad's conversational staples. And women too, of course, Tamas Black being the self-proclaimed expert on that particular subject. No woman in Fife could be considered 'fit for it' until she had figured on the list of those whom Tamas would most like to 'shunt' if he ever got the chance some dark night on his way home after a bevvy or two.

"Kenny," I said, "were you really in a battle in 1915?"

" 'In a battle?' " he said. "By Christ, lad, I was in two o' the fucking things that year."

Slowly the rest of the squad zombied ahead of us, dragging their feet. Fredo paused, lowered his sack, prodded a suspicious-looking Dell with his stick and moved on without pulling it out. Kenny stood in his drill with his eagle eye turned inward.

"What's today's date?" he said.

Five miles away a train steamed out of Fife onto the Tay Bridge, trailing grey smoke as it chuntered towards Dundee on the far shore, its sprawl of windows winking in the sun. The heat of high summer beat down on the back of my neck, reminding me of my insignificance in the wider scheme of things. The steady, unrelenting pace of the roguing, step after step, drill after drill, round after round, was imposing its rhythm. Murtry and its fields was a world unto itself. Could it be Wednesday?

"Maybe it's July the first," I guessed.

"Ah," said Kenny. "Well now. Let's see. We had the Battle o' Neuve Chapelle first, for a warm-up. That was in March, 1915. Then we had the Battle o' Loos after that, September the 25th. That's when we went over the top. *Nemo me impune lacessit*. Do you know what that means, College?"

Nemo: no-one. *Me*: me. *Impune*: by, with or from impunity. *Lacessit*: will attack. No-one attacks me with impunity.

"Correct," said Kenny. "I'm glad to see it's the proper Latin you're getting at that there university down the road from here."

He balanced the sharp end of his stick under the swelling flower buds of a Pentland Dell.

"Fifty years ago today," said Kenny, "we'd have been in Laventie most probably, our squad. Or somewhere thereabouts. Rest they called it. Fucking rest! In that fucking war you worked twice as hard in Rest as you did in the fucking trenches."

He gazed at the end of his stick, looking inward and back.

"Fifty years is a long time when you think about it, College. *Tempus fugit,* and no mistake. I'll tell you one thing, though. If we hadn't had your Muzzie-boys alongside us at Loos, we might have lost the whole damned show. Seriously. They fought like fuck for us, they did. Windy, my arse. They were as brave as the brave until they lost their officers. That's what dished us all in the end. The system was wrong, see. As soon as the officers went down we was fucked – no orders, no battle, no chance."

Muzzie-boys at Loos. Had I known that? Or had I forgotten?

"What was it like?" I said.

"'Like'?" said Kenny. "It was a war, lad, that's what it was like. There's no comparison."

"I mean, what happened out there? With you and the Muzzie-boys. At the Battle of Loos?"

Kenny frowned and looked away.

"There were thousands o' them," he said. "They wore these big fucking turbans on their heads. *'Teek hai,* Johnny, *Alleyman no bon.'* Christ, we couldn't understand a word they said until they started swearing. *'Ally veet, fuck you, bully beef compree?'* "

There were no Hindus or Muslims in the war poems Megan and Jannat had underlined in 'Up The Line To Death' yet apparently there had been thousands of them.

"Thousands?" I said. "You mean literally thousands?"

"Christ lad," said Kenny, "do you think I'm making it up? There were tens of thousands of them out there, a whole army. And thank God. I wouldn't be here today if there'd been no Muzzzie-boys at Loos and that's the God's honest truth."

The rest of the squad were miles ahead in their drills by this stage. With a flick of his stick Kenny returned to the present tense. Decapitated Dell blossoms went flying in all directions. We hoisted our sacks and moved on.

4 HOME FIT FOR HEROES

In the space of two generations the Morrison family's dedication to the potato had raised them from the tenantry to the squirearchy. Davy held the home farm at Lower Murtry; Big John was next door at Wester Murtry; Hector Morrison had Pittendrie Top, three miles away on the big hill. Having ceded the actual growing to his three boys, the patriarch, Auld Andy Morrison, now concentrated on stitching together the big deals with the English growers on which the family fortune prospered. Auld Andy was a power in the land, agriculturally speaking. He was always roaring off in his Jaguar on some important errand, leaving Davy to handle the roguing. Half-acrown per hour was our basic wage, minus the five shillings per day board and lodging, plus a bonus at the end of the season. Board was provided by Wilma at the Murtry big house, except at weekends. Our lodging was a disused cottage by the track that led to the old jetty on the Tay bankside. Fredo had christened it the Wank Hut and the name stuck. The kitchen's amenities comprised a single brass tap and a double gas ring for cooking on. The lavatory was outside. Its door was attached by half a hinge and a twist of orange baler twine. The nearest pub was four miles away in the little burgh of New Buildings.

"Go if you want," said Fredo, tugging off his wellies. "I'm staying here. I'm done in."

He was right. A four-mile hike for a pint of beer was out of the question. We were blistered and sore. Slumped on the doorstep, I recognised Kenny heading our way along the far edge of the field. He had his fishing rod with him, tied in a canvas wrap.

"You'll give yourself a headache, lads," he said, indicating Fredo's Sputniki transistor radio, "listening to that kind o' racket without earplugs."

"It's called music," said Fredo.

"If that's what you call music, son, what would you call a sack full of cats all at it at once?"

At that stage, the Sixties had not yet started to swing in north Fife. Nor did anyone we knew have urgent plans to go to San Francisco with flowers in their hair. As far as hair was concerned, Fredo and I parted ours neatly on the left. My roguing jeans were the first pair I had ever owned. That's what jeans were for in 1965 – for working in.

"Is that a packet o' fags you've got there by any chance, young College?"

Cigarettes were good for you. Beer was compulsory. Ninety percent of 19-year olds were virgins by law in 1965, as I was myself. The only thing that had started to swing was the music we listened to on the radio.

'I'm a-gonna love ya nite and day –'

Radio Caroline blared out loud and clear. Fredo frugged his head from side to side.

"Bo Diddely?" said Kenny. "What kind o' fucking name is Bo, for fucksake?"

He picked up the Sputniki and examined its construction.

"Can you no get Herman's Hermits on it somehow?" he said. "Or a wee bit o' that Petunia Clark. She's nice enough."

Were we the first teenagers Kenny had ever come across?

"It's the times," said Fredo. "They are a-changin."

"Aye," said Kenny, "that's plain to see. The question is, do either o' you two saft, wally English bastards fancy a spot o' fishing?"

Fredo declined, pointing to his blisters. Kenny was not sympathetic.

"When you've marched fourteen miles with a full pack on your back and two hundred extra ball in your webbing," he snorted, "that's when you can talk to me about blisters, young Fredo. How about you, College? Fancy some fishing?"

I had intended to save the best of the evening for bringing my diary up to date. On the other hand, I was always susceptible to a manly new pursuit.

"*Tray bon*," said Kenny. "Hoist your hype then, our College."

* * * * *

Murtry's old boat lay upside down by the rotting pier, tied to an aspen tree. She was called Iris, for reasons Kenny could no longer recall. We shoved her in with a muddy splash and she carried us upstream, letting in water through cracked ribs each time we shifted position. Kenny's tackle box opened like a jewellery case. He spliced an orange and black spinner to his line and kicked towards me the buckled old paint tin that served as a baler. Iris wobbled on her keel.

"Steady she goes, College."

Kenny rose carefully to the upright position while I gripped both sides of the boat to brace it. The tiger-striped lure whizzed through the air and plopped out of sight. I set the oars and began to pull. After ten minutes I was breathing hard while Kenny's reeled-in lure dangled emptily, dripping gold and silver droplets back into the river.

"Salmon – one," I said, "tiger – nil."

Tay-water slopped around our ankles. I shipped oars clumsily and scraped with the baler.

"Wheesht!" hissed Kenny. "Yon salmon'll hear ye." The choice, I pointed out, was to bale or sink.

"Or you can do it yourself," I said, "if you think you're in such fine fettle."

Kenny cackled and coughed and rolled us both one of his famously thin cigarettes. On the Murtry shore, clean tea-towels hung on Wilma's clothes' line like a naval signal in cipher. Nothing moved, barely a ripple.

"Think you're ready for a go with the lure?" said Kenny.

I selected a blue and silver one and stood up to make my first cast. By some fluke my lure sailed high and wide instead of its hook snagging the back of my breeks. Kenny took the oars and pulled us upriver towards Kilspindle. He was in the middle of telling me how the Morrisons were renting two fields off the farmer there for a crop of Majestics when suddenly – *whump!* – the rod quivered in my hands.

"I've got one!"

"Keep it up for fucksake!" The line went slack.

"I said *up*," said Kenny, snatching the rod from me. "We've got him!"

"What do you mean," I said, "*we've* got him'? *I* got him."

"Fair play," said Kenny, reeling furiously. "Let's just call it teamwork."

As the salmon's strength began to ebb, Kenny motioned me to get ready with the landing net. Spitting profanities, he whacked it with his gaff and the salmon's life seeped away, staining the bubbles in the bottom of the boat with a pinkish tinge. He declared it to be a twelve pounder at least. We beached on the spit of gravel below Camras and heaved Iris up the bank and keeled her over. The salmon lay with one glass eye staring up at nothing. It was the biggest thing I had ever killed in my life.

"Christ, College," said Kenny, "it's a fish for fucksake. You don't kill a fish, it's food."

We climbed the hill and took the back way to the Factor's Lodge where Kenny lived. We splashed our fishy hands under the scullery tap and dried them on a couple of tea-towels that seemed remarkably fresh and well laundered.

"Glasses over there," said Kenny, meaning the pantry.

The top shelf was full of tinned food – Spam, rice pudding and peaches in syrup. The bottom shelf held the cups and glasses, and a jar of Robertson's strawberry jam with a golliwog on the label.

"Here's to a fine catch, College."

We sat in the parlour on either side of the cold hearth with the whisky between us.

"Beginner's luck," I replied.

Dried birds' nests and the bleached skulls of several small mammals decorated the mantel shelf. There were few books, nor did Kenny possess a television.

"I watch it down at the big house if there's a need," he said, "same as the telephone. Telly's fine for the bairns like, but who wants to sit in front o' a fucking box all night instead o' playing dominoes?"

He topped up his glass and then mine.

"That was a fine beast we caught tonight," he said. "You did well for a first-timer. How old are you anyway? Nineteen? Damned fine age. You're fit for anything at nineteen."

Kenny mellowed under the liquor's influence. I sipped carefully and tried to hold my own. Something about me – despite the obvious discrepancies – appealed to him.

"Hold it right there, College," he said. "I've got something to show you."

Drawers banged open and shut in his bedroom across the hallway.

"Come in here, son," he called. "You'll find this interesting if you're interested in the war."

Kenny's bedroom was furnished with a bed, a chest of drawers and two nails in the back of the door for hanging things from. The nails were empty. Kenny's spare cardigan hung from the end of his iron bedstead.

"I haven't had this out for a while," he murmured. "Not for a long, long while."

On his knees was a biscuit tin with a thatched cottage depicted on its lid. One by one he extracted his relics from within and spread them out, a hackle of red feathers from his Army bonnet, a scrap of chain mail about two inches square ... and three medals with their rainbow ribbons entangled.

"Pip, Squeak and Wilfred," he said. "They gave these three out willy nilly when the war was over."

The silver medal showed a ploughboy on a carthorse, trampling Germany's eagled shield into the soil of Flanders. Kenny's name was stamped into the rim of it: 13481 Pte K Roberts R Hlndrs. His photographs were at the bottom of the heap, mixed up with postcards of Kodakcolour holidays.

"That's us," he said, pointing with his cracked thumb nail. "That's me. And that's our Billy."

It was a studio portrait with a deckled edge. A squad of Scottish soldiers stood in their khaki drab against a screen painted like a rose bower. Kenny was wearing a tartan-less kilt, thick woollen socks and a pair of boots too big for him.

"That's what I looked like, College, at nineteen years old."

Kenny identified each member of his squad by name: Sergeant Ross; Pal Duncan; Wee Sammy Chisholm; Our Billy.

"He was my best pal was Billy Rankin," said Kenny. "His Pa had the forge up at Crean."

Our Billy's square features suggested a young soldier who was ready. Sergeant Ross stood half a head higher than the rest, chin in, chest out. Wee Sammy looked a proper little rascal. The photograph was actually a postcard, with room on the back for a message and address. There was no message.

'*Studio Deglasse, Rue Voltaire, Bethune.*'

"We had to pay for fifty o' these things," said Kenny, "and we hardly sent off half o' them between the four of us. Christ, that came as a surprise, when we realised we hardly knew more than a dozen folk in the whole wide world. I gave one o' mine to a tart in the Red Lamp at Bethune."

Ribbons and rosettes from ploughing competitions lay on Kenny's quilt in dredged clumps knotted with trinkets. By 'Red Lamp' he meant a military brothel.

"Red Lamps were for the Other Ranks," said Kenny, "Blue Lamps for the officers. There were whole battalions queuing up for a go at it before the Battle o' Loos. The M.P.s were there to keep 'em in line – cavalry, infantry, our boys, your boys."

"The Muzzie-boys?"

"Oh yes. The Army was very democratic that way," said Kenny. "All a man needed for a French woman was the cash. And your Muzzie-boys were partial to a bit of white rabbit by all accounts. Five *frong* for a jiggy-jig, ten *frong* if you wanted a whole quarter-hour at it. The whore that picked me was so glaikit when she opened her legs I near heaved up my dinner. I gave her the five *frong* and did the business then chucked her one o' these here photos to mind me by. We had some high old times did me and Billy afore the Battle o' Loos. *San fairy ann, Mamselle*, and out the fucking door *toot sweet*!"

The last relic to come out of the biscuit tin was a tarnished metal capsule for holding pen nibs. It rolled in Kenny's palm like a seed pod. "A-ha! This is what I wanted to show you."

Inside was a scroll of torn-off paper, written in blue pencil in a language that looked like a row of squashed weevils.

"Now then," said Kenny, "would you do me the honour of reading that for me, kind sir."

My heart sank. Kenny leaned forward expectantly, blocking the twilight gathering outside his window.

"I can't read this," I said.

Kenny reached for the light switch.

"No," I said. "I mean, I don't understand it."

"It's in that there Indi-lingo," said Kenny.

There were three short lines of weevil words and then what might have been a signature. The only possible clue was in the message's closing bracket: '(Ali Haidar, naik, 58 V.R.)'.

"I told you," I said. "I am not a Muzzie-boy. I'm English."

I was not the *pukka* woggie Kenny needed. English was my mother tongue. It had never occurred to anyone in Lichfield, including myself, that my father's half of my inheritance might ever come in handy.

"What is it?" I said.

"I don't know," said Kenny, taking back the scrip between two fingers. "Some kind o' souvenir. It was on me when I woke up wounded. The padre found it tucked in my button hole. Battle o' Loos, College. September 25th, 1915."

"Is that where you got your shoulder?"

Kenny straightened his stoop.

"Aye, lad. That's where I got my shoulder."

I suggested that (58 V.R.) might be something to do with Queen Victoria.

"It means Vaughan's Rifles I reckon," said Kenny. "There was a mob o' Vaughans in the same brigade as us. Punjabis they were called. It must have been one o' them. You'd stick your name and number on a man if you brought him in wounded, for the reward like. He was meant to reward you somehow."

On September 25th, 1915, at the Battle of Loos, one Ali Haidar, an Indian soldier and presumed Punjabi Muslim, had found the 19year old Kenny Roberts on the battlefield, wounded and unconscious, and brought him in. Fifty years on, Kenny sat on the edge of his bed wondering why I couldn't help.

"Would you like me to try my mother?" I said. "She might know someone."

It was the best I could offer.

"That'd be grand, lad," said Kenny, brightening, "if you could manage that for me."

He rolled up his scrip and handed it to me in its pellet. Then he re-packed his biscuit tin.

'Huntley & Palmers. De Luxe Selection.'

It was a home fit for heroes, that thatched cottage in its garden. Children danced and played on an emerald lawn spread for a picnic, unaware of the black dog hiding in the hollyhocks.

5 IN THE TRENCH

The biggest field we ever rogued as a full squad was at Lenzie Mains near Glenfarg where the Morrisons rented 43 acres for a crop of Pentland Javelin that turned out to be minging with blackleg. It took two whole days to finish the first roguing at Lenzie, plus part of the following morning. Tamas threw himself down after the last round with a theatrical display of exhaustion.

"That's it boys," he announced. "I'm dead. Box up my coffin."

He had started the day with a bad hangover and wanted to take the piece break early to sleep it off. Kenny, however, wanted to quit Lenzie *toot sweet* so we could take the measure of Big John's Dell back at Wester Murtry.

"Tamas, for fucksake," he pleaded, "now's not the time for kipping."

The rest of us gathered at the van to share the last of the bottle of Irn Bru. Fredo wiped the top of the bottle, doctor-style, to spread the germs around more hygienically.

"Aw,Kenny," groaned Tamas. "I'm fucking shattered, man."

"We're all fucking shattered," replied Kenny. "It's what we get paid for."

He gave Tamas a prod with his stick. Tamas swiped at him. Kenny gave him another prod. Tamas rose to his knees. That's when he saw me, sitting in the front seat of the van glugging down the Bru.

"Oi, you!" he roared. "Out o' my seat right now, you black, woggie bastard."

"I beg your pardon?"

"I said OUT!" bellowed Tamas. "That's my seat."

His thrown roguing stick hit the side of the van with a thump. Shane picked it up and stood to attention wagging his tail.

"I've told you, Tamas," I said, "Woggie is not my name. Bastard is not my name. You fuck-faced Scottish arsehole."

Even I was taken aback. Tamas blazed his Viking-blue eyes at me on full power. *Fuck-faced Scottish arsehole?* The squad stood rooted in amazement.

"I'm giving you one last chance," said Tamas grimly, "before I come over there and knock you right out o' my seat."

"Come on then," I said. "Come and knock me out of your seat. Then what?"

In the silence that followed I heard larks. Wee Eck looked at me with big round eyes. He had never seen a woggie bastard asking for a good kicking before. I took off my specs. Tamas showed me his fist. I handed my folded specs to Fredo.

Everyone knew I had no chance. The best I could hope for was to get in a few kicks of my own before I went under. I blinked shortsightedly, playing for the sympathy vote. There could be no backing down. Tamas offered me one last chance.

"Am I going to have to drag you out o' my seat by the scruff o' your neck," he said, "or are you going to hand it over nice and friendly like?"

That's when the unthinkable happened. Bender pushed me sideways on the seat and hitched himself up into the van in my place. Then it was Tamas' turn to blink.

"Have you gone saft in the head, Ben?" he said. "Or what?"

"Mebbe I have gone saft in the head," said Bender. "Or mebbe it's just that I'm just seeing things logical like. See, what if this here bit o' front seat I'm in is no your bit o' front seat at all, Tamas? What then?"

"Fuck off. Of course it's my seat. Who else's bit o' front seat could it be?"

"What if," said Bender, concentrating hard, "what if it's my bit o' front seat? I mean, if College here is sitting in my bit o' front seat that means I must be sitting on yours. That's logical. So, then. What are you going to do about it?"

No one in his right mind would pick a fight with Bender no matter what kind of twisted logic came out his mouth. At the age of fourteen, at the Freuchie Highland Games, he had bent a horse shoe out of true and won a fiver for it. That's why he was called Bender. There was nothing he could not bend with his bare hands except, perhaps, a tractor axle. Tamas frowned. He sensed that the mood of the squad had turned against him.

"You *cunts!*"

First Wee Eck; then Kenny; now Bender. All three had decided to like me and Fredo. They had made a space in the squad for us. I nudged Bender to show I was happy to slide into the back of the van now that he'd made my point for me. He responded by wedging me firmly into place with his right buttock.

"You stay there," he said. "You've got your seat, now sit in it."

Kenny opened the van's rear doors for Tamas to get in the back way but he stayed where he was. Shane jumped up instead, wagging his tail and bestowing wet licks.

"You're all cunts," raged Tamas, "nicking my front seat."

"Calm yourself down, son," said Kenny. "He's one o' us, for fucksake, our College. They're alright, him and Fredo. Let's away to Big John's Dell and no hard feelings, eh?"

Tamas hurled his sack into the back of the van and climbed in after it using his elbows and knees to deliver vengeance. I turned in my front seat and handed over my packet of Regals as a peace offering. Fredo lit his fag and held out the cupped flame to Tamas.

"Hurry up," he said, "before I burn myself."

"Burn then," snarled Tamas, "you fucking, poofy English bastard."

* * * * *

Big John's two fields of Dell revealed themselves as big squares of brown and green stripes running down to the Tay shore. At the crest of Crean Law, Kenny cut the Bedford's engine and we coasted down the brae to Wester Murtry with the wind in our hair. Alongside the tatties were the Morrisons' long, thin fields of raspberries and strawberries. The white figures flitting about were the berry pickers, women and children brought in by bus each day from Dundee. Kenny's first impressions was not good.

"There's rogues in here somewhere," he fretted, "and they'll be Desiree. I guarantee it."

Desiree was the new wonder potato from Holland. She had a lilac-purple blossom and a good-sized pink tuber. The English growers had taken to her because she was a heavy cropper and matured quickly.

"You're wrong Kenny," said Bender. "There'll be no rogues here. It was further along that Big John had his tatties three years ago. There'll be no rogues here unless he mixed up his seed."

The men and boys of Murtry carried in their heads the history of every field they had ever worked. Kenny and Bender soon had Big John's crop rotation worked out: tatties; peas; neeps; then barley; *then* tatties again. The excitement was all too much for Tamas.

"See me," he said, "I'm off up yonder to get some o' them berries down me."

He lobbed the crust of his last piece at Shane and trailed off towards the berry field. Bender and Wee Eck guzzled to the end of another shared bottle of 'Irn Bru' – it was Wee Eck's Bru, Bender had kindly offered to share it – then they too drifted berry-wards. Fredo rolled onto his side and shut his eyes. Kenny passed me something he'd spotted in Bender's 'Daily Record'. It was the photograph of an American soldier in Vietnam, down on one knee throwing a hand grenade. 'The Marine Corps under pressure,' said the caption, 'north of Qang Tri.'

"He's keeping low," explained Kenny, "so he doesn't present a target. Proper bombing's for close quarters, for fighting from traverse to traverse, the way we did it."

I had no clear notion of what a traverse might be.

"Come here, for fucksake," sighed Kenny, marching me to the endrig for a lesson in war-craft.

He dragged a line in the dirt with the point of his roguing stick, the length of a tennis court. Then he drew another line, parallel to the first.

"Right," he said, standing between his two drawn lines, "imagine this is your actual trench right here that I'm standing in. Six foot deep if you're lucky, or maybe five at the Battle o' Loos, including the height o' the parapet and the two feet o' mud at the bottom."

Kenny stood me at one end of his imaginary trench and went down to the other end.

"Now then, imagine I'm a big fucking Jerry," he said, turning to face me from the distance of about thirty feet. "Imagine I've just got into your trench with a squad o' mates. If your trench has been dug in a straight line like this, you and *your* mates – you're fucked. One volley from Old Jerry and it's *napoo* the lot o' you."

Defending a long, straight trench against an enemy inside it would certainly have presented a problem, I could see that.

"So what we did was," said Kenny, "we put in traverses."

Kenny went to the middle of his drawn tram lines and erased about ten feet of them, drawing in a kink at right angles before joining it up again.

"Reckon you can see me now," he said, "now that we've put in a traverse?"

Kenny crouched in his imaginary traverse and poked his head round its corner. He ducked out of sight and popped back again.

"See what I'm saying? If your trench is straight, everyone in it is a target. Mix in a couple o' traverses and you're protected."

Kenny went over to the nearest pile of shaws and gathered up some grenade-sized tatties.

"And that's why you need bombs."

Kenny stood me on one side of his imaginary traverse and pressed down on my shoulders until I was in an ape-like crouch. I smelled the battle juice on his breath. He shoved a couple of tatties into my hands and skittered up the trench to take up a position out of sight in his imaginary traverse.

"Remember," he said, "I'm a big, fat Jerry and you can't see me. You're on that side o' the traverse and I'm on this one. So, College. How are you going to kill me?"

Bombs, of course. lobbed over the top.

"Right," said Kenny. "Off you go."

"What?"

"Go on. Bomb me. I'm a Ger-boy. You want to kill me. You *have* to kill me."

I lobbed a potato bomb in Kenny's direction. As soon as it was in the air he dived out of his imaginary traverse and threw his own bomb. While my bomb landed harmlessly in the empty traverse Kenny's bomb skimmed off my shoulder.

"Tough luck, son," he said. "That's your head off."

"That's not fair. I wasn't expecting it."

That made him laugh.

"Fair?" he said. "Of course it's not fair. I'm a Jerry. I want to kill you by fair means or foul."

Kenny pressed me back into the ape shape again. This time he gave me his stick to hold, diagonally across my chest.

"Right," he said. "This time, College, you're the bayonet man. Rifle at the port, bayonet fixed. Your finger is on the trigger guard mind, *not* on the trigger. We don't want anything going off by mistake in the heat o' the moment. Are you ready?"

"What for?"

"For the traverse, you saft wally bastard. Pay attention. Remember, Old Jerry is in your trench and heading towards you. If you don't get into that traverse from your side before he gets into it from his side – you're fucked. So. You are the bayonet man. I am the bomber, right behind you. As soon as I chuck this bomb you charge into the traverse and stab or shoot any bastard who stands in your way. Go for his throat or his kidneys. Go for his bollocks. For God's sake don't go for his ribs. If your sword gets stuck in his ribs you'll never get it out again."

"I thought we were both bombers?"

"We are, lad. I'm showing you how a bomb squad works up a trench – bayonet man, bomber, bayonet man, bomber. You take it in turns, see."

"So why can't I chuck the bomb and you stab the German?"

"Because the best bomber is always Number One and the third best bomber is always his bayonet man. And in this squad, that's you."

Kenny showed me his potato bombs.

"Ready?"

"But I'm a bowler. I want to chuck bombs."

"Shut up. I'm in charge. You're the bayonet man. Get moving."

Kenny crouched down behind me with his bombs at the ready. In my mind's eye I could see a hulking great Jerry on the other side of the traverse, waiting for me with his rifle and bayonet. Kenny pressed his finger to his lips. I balanced on the balls of my feet. All my senses were on alert. I tightened my grip on my rifle. It was ridiculous.

"Strike first," growled Kenny, "strike sure."

He had a bomb in each hand. As soon as I gave the signal he was going to throw them. What was the signal? I raised my eyebrows. Kenny nodded. He pulled back his straight arm. As soon as his bomb was in the air I was going to charge into the traverse and stab or shoot any fucking Jerry who got in my way –

"Hey! You two daft bastards," called Tamas. "What do you think you're playing at? Come and see what your nice Uncle Tamas has got for you."

He was swinging a plastic bucket by its handle. The walls of Kenny's trench at the Battle of Loos evaporated.

"Ah," he said. "That's a damned lucky let off for Jerry, that is. Saved by the bell. We'd have had him for sure, College."

He lobbed his bombs harmlessly into the nettles on the other side of the endrig and took one of the proffered strawberries from Tamas' pail.

"You should see the talent up in that there berry field," said Tamas. "Why the hell did you no tell us Miss Jane was back from college, Kenny? Christ, even a poofy English bastard like you, College, would get a cock-stand seeing the fine, ripe jugs hanging off of the front of Miss Jane this year."

"Miss Jane?" said Kenny. "You can forget Miss Jane, Tamas Black. She's being plumped up for some young gent with a thousand acres or more to his name. If Big John Morrison catches the likes o' you sniffing round his precious Jane, he'll set his dogs on you for sure."

Kenny snapped his fingers and Shane came obediently to heel from wherever he'd been hiding. Fredo yawned and stretched after his kip.

"Aye but," said Tamas stubbornly, "she gave me a look did she no, Bender?"

"Did she fuck," said Bender through a mouthful of strawberry pulp. "Who the fuck would give you a look, for fucksake? Yon Jane wouldn't let you near her wi' a bargepole."

We finished the strawberries and lined up in squad order. No amount of argument about the fabled Miss Jane could distract Kenny when there was a job of work waiting to be done.

"There's rogues in here, lads," he said. "I can smell 'em. The first one that gets me a Desiree this afternoon gets the florin."

We rogued to the top of the field without mishap and emptied our sacks of shaws in the endrig. Then, at Tamas' beckoning, we crept to the thin screen of saplings that had been planted as a windbreak and peered through.

"What do you make o' that lads?"

The berry field on the other side was full of bright chatter. Women and children were working their way down each row of berries, picking one section clean before moving on to the next. When their plastic buckets were full they carried them to the trestles at the far end of the field for weighing and paying.

"Wheesht!" said Tamas. "There she is –"

A girl in jeans and T-shirt bounced into view and climbed onto a fork-lift truck stacked with cardboard punnets. She dropped off the punnets by the weighing machine and drove towards us.

"What are you hiding over there for, you boys?" she called out.

"Hello, Kenny."

"Good afternoon, Miss Jane."

She was a fantasy of honeyed loveliness. Her thick auburn hair glistened in the sun. Her brown eyes shone. Miss Jane's confident posture astride the fork-lift displayed her every asset to perfection.

Fredo made an involuntary noise at the back of his throat.

"I didn't know the roguing had started," she said.

"Oh aye," said Kenny. "And the boys here are getting their eye in at long last."

I racked my brains for something clever to say but nothing came. Bender and Tamas gawped gormlessly. Fredo just stood there. Having accomplished her purpose – to see with her own eyes the saft, wally English bastards she'd heard so much about – Miss Jane turned back to her work.

"I'll be meeting Lizzie Purdom up at The Brig on Friday night, Bender," she said, "if you fancy popping along."

"I certainly fancy popping something," muttered Tamas.

Bender tried to say something but like the rest of us, he had been struck dumb. Nor was Miss Jane the only excitement of the afternoon. We were hardly half way back down the tattie field when Wee Eck let out a yell.

"Boys! Kenny! See here!"

He had found a handsome, dark-leafed potato with a pronounced purple vein in its stem, quite different from the white-flowering Pentland Dell. It was a Desiree – our first proper rogue of the season.

"Good spot, Eckie!" said Kenny, grudgingly fishing out his florin. "I told you boys. I *knew* there was Desiree in this lot."

Wee Eck glowed with quiet pride. Bender slapped him on the back, which must have hurt. Our very first rogue! Pretty soon we had all got one of our own. It took another couple of rounds for the full horror to dawn on us.

"This crop's *minging* with Desiree," said Tamas, casting his arm wide. "It'll take us all year to get through this lot."

"The sooner it's done," said Kenny, stiffening his entire posture, "the sooner it's done."

The last round of the day took us a whole hour to finish. If the rest of Big John's Dell had the same amount of Desiree rogues in it, we were looking at a mountain of work.

"It's way worse than Lenzie," said Tamas gloomily.

"Aye," said Bender, "but there is that view o' the berry field to cheer us on our way."

"That Miss Jane," said Fredo, "she is a goddess."

"Oi!" said Tamas. "Hands off our Miss Jane. That's the prime o' Fife talent you're talking about, Fredo. A saft wally English bastard like you is not equipped for the kind o' shunting *she* needs."

Fredo merely smiled. It was love at first sight, between him and Miss Jane, although no one knew that at the time.

6 MUD

For as long as we were roguing Big John's Dell, Kenny and the boys walked to work early each morning, leaving the Bedford van in its stable and collecting me and Fredo at the Wank Hut on the way to the field. It was established policy in the squad to rogue in gruff silence until the morning's first fag break. On our third day in the Dell, we were squatting in a corner of the field with our smokes when Bender spied the berry bus coming down the brae.

"What time o' day do you call this to be starting work?" he boomed. "Get your jugs out, Janey," shouted Tamas, "and give us all a thrill."

Since our first encounter with Miss Jane in the berry field she had become a shared obsession. Fredo explained it by reference to the influence of the female *mammae* on the workings of the male endocrine system. Bender and Tamas put it in cruder terms. She waved innocently from the open door of the berry bus.

"Tell Wullie to keep the revs up," shouted Kenny.

Wullie Sharp was Lower Murtry's all purpose driver-mechanic.

"He'll lose it for sure," said Wee Eck, "if he tries to take the gate at that speed."

Right enough, Wullie Sharp lost it at the Wester Murtry gate. The engine stalled and the berry bus lurched to a halt with its back end blocking the lane.

"He'll still be half-pished from The Brig last night," said Kenny.

"Wullie Sharp," hollered Tamas, "you're a fucking disgrace."

"Mind your fucking language," scolded Kenny. "There's bairns on yon bus, for fucksake."

We flicked our smoked fags into the hedge and turned our attention to Big John's Dell once more and finished the round. An uneasy quiet prevailed. The wide River Tay lay clamped under a lid of grey cloud.

"Aye, there's a heap o' weather on its way," predicted Kenny.

Half way through the next round, a Biblical bolt of lightning cracked the sky, followed by another. An onrush of wind brought the first, fat raindrops splashing down and sent the berry pickers in the next field stampeding for shelter. Kenny and the boys slicked on the rubberised waterproofs they had tied around their waists as a precaution. Fredo and I were soaked through to the skin within seconds. Kenny took pity and sent us back to the farm to get waterproofs and to bring the Bedford van back with us. The lads rogued on, professionally oblivious to the downpour. They were a squad. It took more than a spot of rain to put them off their stride. At midday, we piled into the van like a pack of dogs, scattering droplets. Shane, of course, had to stay out in the wet, underneath.

"Fucking mud," said Bender, flicking some from off his piece.

"Mud you call it," said Kenny, unwrapping his own piece. "Christ, you boys don't know what real mud is."

We all had a pudding-sized clodge of mud on each wellied foot. It felt real enough. Plus, our faces and hair were daubed with it.

"Mud?" said Kenny. "Nah. That's just a wee bit o' dirt. Real mud comes up to your waist."

"Aw, Christ!" groaned Tamas. "Here you go again, Kenny. Can you not shut up for once about you and your bastard war? We're sick o' hearing about it."

"I'm not," I said.

Having learned a little of what Kenny knew about throwing bombs I still didn't know half-enough of what had happened at the Battle of Loos with him and the Muzzie-boys.

"When we were in the Salient," he said, "one o' our blokes got stuck in the mud for sixty-five hours and that's the God's honest truth because the Adjutant was there and he timed it. We tied the poor bastard to a mule to drag him out and the fucking mule sank with him. We had to leave them both behind."

A Spam piece and a cheese piece with pickle on it comprised the un-varying ingredients of Kenny's lunch, followed by an apple, followed by a fag and a nip or two of battle juice.

"You left them?" said Fredo. "You left them in the mud?"

"Wheesht and let me finish," said Kenny.

He untwisted the paper plug from the neck of his 'Old Grouse' whisky bottle and took a slug.

"The relief got them out in the end," he said. "Fuck knows how, but they did. Our bloke turned up at billets the next day with two sandbags wrapped round his feet and half his vest hanging off. Everything else had come away in the mud. I forget his name but I saw him once in Cowdenbeath after the war. He was lucky alright, damned lucky. We lost plenty like that, in the mud."

"Cowdenbeath?" sniffed Bender. "What's lucky about that?"

I liked hearing Kenny talk about his war. I felt almost jealous to have been born too late for it. The more he talked about it the more I seemed to remember things I could never have known. Wilfred

Owen was part of my English birthright, along with those Muzzie-boys who'd saved Kenny's bacon at the Battle of Loos.

" 'Bent double', " I said, " 'like old beggars under sacks, knock-kneed, coughing like hags, we cursed through sludge, till on the haunting flares we turned out backs, and towards our distant rest began to trudge ...' "

"You what?" said Bender.

"Wheesht, Ben," said Kenny, "and pin back your lug-holes. You carry on with your pomes, young College. I like 'em."

"Sorry," I said. "I think that's all I can remember." "Thank fuck for that," said Tamas.

" 'Men marched asleep,' " said Fredo, taking up the theme. " 'Many had lost their boots, but limped on, blood-shod ...' tum-titty, tumtitty ... 'Gas! Gas! Quick, boys! An ecstasy of fumbling ...' and then something, something, something ... 'like a man in fire or lime' ..."

"Like a man in fire or *lime*?" said Bender. "Would you two mind telling us just what the fuck it is you're blethering on about?"

"Didn't you do the war poets?" said Fredo. "At school?"

Bender gawped at the crazy notion that anyone might seek to fondly remember in later years anything learned at school.

"Wilfred Owen?" I said. " 'Dulce Et Decorum Est'?"

"Aye," said Kenny. "That's the Latin for it."

"The Latin for what exactly," sneered Tamas, "I say chaps, jolly good weather for cricket, what?' "

"It is a fine and fitting thing," I said, "to die for your country."

"Gobshite!" said Tamas. "Only a half-English bastard could say that and mean it."

"How do you mean, gobshite?" said Kenny quietly.

He wiped his chin with back of his hand and twisted the paper plug back into his bottle and then pierced Tamas through with his gimlet eye. Rain rattled on the van's tin roof and trickled down its windows. Tamas chewed on his piece and stared straight ahead. Bender shifted his weight in his seat, nobody spoke. Sorry was not a word that came easily. If someone hurt your feelings in north Fife you either shut up about it or started a fight. Kenny had fought *pro patria*. Sergeant Ross and Billy had died in the mud of the Western Front for Tamas's right to call their war gobshite. We listened to the rain some more.

"Here's a pome about the war for you, College," said Kenny, clearing his throat. "It's called 'The Piper o' Loos' and it goes like this: 'He piped in Scotia's bonny land, he piped a sweet Strathspey/ He piped in India's coral strand, a Tullochgoram gay/ He piped a war charge when at Loos, he fell yet piped on still/ And while this land shall valour choose, his pipes shall Scotland thrill.' "

"Aye," said Bender. "I like the short ones, Kenny. Who made that one up?"

" 'Made up' ?" said Kenny. "That's not a made up pome, it's real. That's your actual Piper Laidlaw, Ben. He stood on the parapet at Loos and blew his pipes while the boys went over. And when he took a bullet in the knee he kept on blowing. Aye, 'Blue Bonnets Over The Border'. He copped a V.C. for that did Danny Laidlaw."

"If you like the short ones, Ben," said Tamas, "you'll love this: 'There was an auld maid o' Dundee/ Whose cunt-hairs came down to her knee/ She was brassy and bold/ but at eighty year old/ couldn't give it to sailors for free.' "

Laughter over the makings of Kenny's cigarette turned into another of his epic expectorations.

"You boys," he gasped. "What did I do wrong to get lumbered with a squad o' heathens like you lot? Eh?"

He wound down his window and spat his product into the rain.

"You're coughing well today," said Fredo. "Must be the damp."

"Damp my arse," said Kenny. "I've told you, it's the gas. It's all still in there, Fredo. Old Jerry's fucking gas will do for me yet, you'll see."

* * * * *

We ploughed on and on, up and down Big John's Dell for the rest of that week – two drills apiece, round after round, hour after hour, hauling out Desiree rogue after Desiree rogue, filling our sacks and dumping the shaws then filling them up some more. The rain seeped through the seams of our waterproofs and soaked us. The mud slowed us to a knock-kneed, bent-backed trudge.

" 'All plants need sun and water,' " quoted Tamas at the fag break. "Well, we've had the sun and now, sure as eggs is eggs, we've got the water."

The grey weather lasted until Friday morning and then blew over. At half past four in the afternoon we emptied our sacks for the last time.

"I'm confused," said Tamas. "Remind me again, boys – is this a field o' Dell with Desiree rogues in it, or is it a field o' Desiree with Dell rogues in it?"

We were a weary, stained and filthy squad but as Bender so rightly said: "Fuck it. It's pay day."

Davy Morrison's office had been built inside the echoing space of Lower Murtry's big new barn. Davy received our bitter assessment of Wester Murtry's Dell without comment. Desiree rogues were not his problem, they were our problem. When the last of the paying-off was done, Davy locked away his cash box and Lower Murtry was at rest for the weekend. Up in the barn's high girders, Wilma's white doves said *coo-coo*.

"Are you ready for The Brig then, lads?" said Tamas, flapping his brown envelope of cash.

"Last one there buys the first round," said Bender, heading towards the corner of the barn where he kept his motorbike under a tarpaulin to protect it from the doves.

Wee Eck waved goodbye and disappeared round the corner with his Dad's arm around his shoulder. The rest of us piled into the souped-up Ford Anglia in which Tamas commuted to and from Gunnie each day. Tamas got us out of the farm gate in the lead but it wasn't much of a race after that. Bender stayed in our slipstream until the straight at Camras and then pulled ahead with power to spare. He was waiting for us as the Anglia clattered onto the cobbles of New Buildings' market square and came to a halt in front of the Old Brig Tavern.

"What kept you?"

Inside, Kenny ordered his customary pint of McEwans Export and ducked into the lounge to assure the domino school that he would be joining them presently. Bender and Tamas also managed to find people to talk to while the pints were pulled, which left me and Fredo to pay for them.

"Cheers, boys."

I shared out my fags. Kenny removed his puttees and re-tied his boot laces. They were a big part of Kenny's life, his boots. Every five years he got the New Buildings shoe-mender, Alistair Menzies, to make him a new pair exactly like the ones he'd had before.

"Twenty-five bob an acre!" announced Bender, reporting to us a conversation he'd just had with Sandy Gillanders about how much his squad was getting paid for roguing Kenny Reid's stuff up at Balcraig. "Sandy burst out laughing when I told him what Davy was paying us again this year."

"Sandy Gillanders?" said Kenny. "That boy couldn't tell a King Edward from his red end."

Tamas set down his glass with a clunk that drew attention to its emptiness.

"Bender's right," he said. "We're diddling ourselves, Kenny. Why rogue for the Morrisons by the hour when Sandy Gillanders can get stuff for twenty-five bob an acre?"

"The roguing's not just about money, son. It's the pride in the job and all."

Fredo returned bearing our second round of pints on a tin tray.

"No, no," insisted Bender. "Roguing's a business, Kenny. You ask Auld Andy. When you're doing business you get the best price you can."

"Forget Sandy Gillanders. We are the squad, Bender. We are *the* squad. *Nemo me impune lacessit*, and don't you forget it."

Tamas drained the second pint that the rest of us had hardly begun and belched and headed for the door.

"I'm off," he said. "It's a big night tonight at Gunnie and them two swifties have set me up nicely for the ride home so thank you kindly, boys."

"Greedy bastard," said Bender.

Without the support of Tamas, Bender's argument with Kenny was lost. He was ruminating on his next gambit when two women entered. Miss Jane spotted us and waved.

"Aw fuck," said Kenny, scraping his chair as he rose to leave, "if the dames have arrived that's the last word o' sense I'll get out o' you boys tonight. I'm off to my doms."

"Aye," said Bender, "fuck off, you tight old bastard. Just when it's your turn to get the next round in."

Miss Jane and her friend finished their debate about whether to join us by deciding that they would.

"Welcome, girls," simpered Bender. "Lovely night for it."

Bender could throw a hammer further than any man in the Old Brig Tavern but his first whiff of Miss Jane's heady perfume had unmanned him completely.

"Lovely night for what exactly?" said Miss Jane's red-haired friend, plonking herself down.

She slid her riding hat and crop under the chair.

"Whatever you fancy, Big Lizzie," said Bender. "A week drink. A wee ride."

"Don't try to be funny, Bender. It doesn't suit you. Aren't you going to introduce us?"

"I certainly am," said Bender. "The woggie here's called College and yon wop is Fredo. Short for Alfie."

"And you must be Lizzie Purdom," I said. "How do you do?"

Big Lizzie had a long freckled face with a strong jaw. Fredo and Miss Jane, I noticed, seemed to require no introduction.

"So," said Miss Jane. "This is nice. How are you new boys finding the roguing this year?"

"We seem to be getting the hang of it," said Fredo. "If in doubt, pull it out.' "

Fredo pronounced it Fife-style: If in doot, pu' it oot. Quoting Kenny's field maxims in his own dialect had become an important part of our double act as saft, wally English bastards. Miss Jane's laughter exposed the whole of her creamy throat. Her lovely *mammae* swelled lusciously. It was too much for Bender.

"Anybody want some crisps?" he gurgled. "I'm feeling a wee bit peckish."

Big Lizzie hitched her chair closer to mine as Bender blundered towards the bar.

"How about yourself, College?" she said. "Can you tell the difference between a Pentland Dell and row of beans yet?"

Big Lizzie helped herself to one of my Regals. I wasn't sure I liked my squad name being used without permission.

"College suits you," she said. "They say you're clever."

It was not necessarily a compliment. 'Not bad at all' was Fife's highest form of praise. 'Clever' implied too clever by half. Big Lizzie upped the wattage of her bright blue eyes.

"What is it you're studying," she said, "down there at St. Andrews?" "Pomes and Fine Art," said Bender, returning with the crisps.

"And what's the use in that?" she said. "Ben, I need more salt on these, please."

I tossed over my salt in its blue twist of waxed paper. It was too noisy in the pub to keep a close ear on what Fredo and Miss Jane were talking about but I had already intuited, with a pang, what the two girls had decided between them about Fredo and me. I prodded my National Health specs back up tp the top of my nose.

"And pomes is not all he's good at," continued Bender, "he's a fucking wizard with his Philosophy. Here, College, what's that one you do about all men are humans therefore all men are wimmin? Something like that. Logic, Lizzie. He can tie you in knots with it."

"And Fredo?" she said. "Is it true he's studying to be a doctor?"

"Oh aye," said Bender, butting in again. "Did you know the bile duct is three inches long? And the male brain is heavier than the female's? He's got yon doctoring right down to his fingertips, our Fredo. He's got one o' them stethy-ma-thingmies down at the Wank Hut."

"The what hut?"

Bender's calf's eyes bulged beneath their blonde lashes.

"The hut," he stammered. "Fredo and College are biding in the old bothy down by the jetty. Excuse me. It's a pish I'm needing."

"Muckle great gallumph," said Big Lizzie as he barged past. "What do you make of them, College?"

I was proud of my hard-earned place in the squad. Brotherhood, beer and fags suited me fine.

" 'Nemo me impune lacessit', " I said. "We're a team."

Close up, Big Lizzie was by no means unappealing to the male endocrine system. Her red hair was in fact copper toned, with gold threads where the sun had caught it.

"Would you like another?" I said, indicating her nearly empty glass of rum and blackcurrant.

"No thanks. We can't leave the horses too long. Come on, Janey. Tear yourself away, girl."

Miss Jane was in no hurry to tear herself away. She and Fredo were getting on like a Wank Hut on fire.

"Come on Jane," she urged, "or you'll be late for your Squash."

"You play Squash?" said Fredo. "Wow. Great. We play it all the time."

It was a lie. Fredo and I had played barely half a dozen games of Squash all year on account of the fact that he was so much better than me and I didn't like losing all the time.

"Great," said Miss Jane, "let's fix up a game. Boys against girls. We've got a court near here – well, a sort of a court – over at the Frasers' place."

Our combined exit was followed by every pair of eyes in the Old Brig Tavern. Bawdy innuendo gusted from the bar as the door latch clunked shut behind us. Miss Jane introduced us to the tethered horses, The Bruce and Macduff. They were huge and terrifying. The Bruce allowed Fredo to stroke his glossy neck. I tried not to look too intimidated.

"Call yourself a cricketer," said Big Lizzie. "Macduff wouldn't hurt a fly."

The girls thanked us again for the drinks we hadn't bought them and Miss Jane fixed up with Fredo to play squash in the very near future. Big Lizzie, I thought, looked rather fine astride her horse. She adjusted a buckle with a firm snap of her wrist. The horses smelled strongly of themselves in the still evening air.

"See you soon then," said Miss Jane.

"Absolutely," said Fredo.

"Hup! *Hup!*" said Big Lizzie.

At the corner of the square, under the green and gold Hovis sign denoting Kennedy's bakery, the girls waved again and disappeared. Fredo and I loitered awhile, looking in the shop windows. New Buildings was provisioned to supply all the necessities but not much else. A bowling green and a drinking fountain erected to celebrate Queen Victoria's jubilee comprised the main civic amenities. By the door of the town's old kirk stood a Celtic cross.

'In memory of the sons of this place who fell in the Great War,
1914 – 1918
George Anderson, Private, Black Watch.
Alexander Black, Private, Black Watch
John Duthie, Bombardier, Royal Field Artillery.'

Behind the lace-curtained windows of the market square families of latter day Andersons and Duthies were mixing their malted milk drinks and preparing for bed. Swifts twitted and swooped over the chimney tops.

James Hastie, Sapper, Royal Engineers.
Walter Kennedy, Private, Black Watch.
William Rankin, Private, Black Watch.

At hearing the call, Billy Rankin had left his father's forge at Crean and gone to France with Kenny and the rest of the ploughboys and had never come back.

'They died that we might live.'

A shop door bell pinged and two grubby boys spilled onto the pavement from Devito's Fish Bar, hungrily unwrapping their chips. "That reminds me," said Fredo. "I'm starving." At that moment, Bender erupted from The Brig.

"Lads, lads! Wait for me!"

He greeted the grubby boys by name and levied a chip off each of them. New Buildings was a small place, not quite a town, perhaps three thousand souls altogether. Everyone knew everyone else. They had given forty-two sons to the war to end War, and another sixteen to the wars that came after.

7 HONOUR

Big John's Dell was the making of our squad. For the necessary purpose of racial denigration Fredo and I would always remain a pair of saft, wally English bastards but our work in Big John's Dell had proved beyond question that we could carry our load. When Fredo jumped the burn between the two fields and twisted his ankle, he kept on roguing. When my blisters burst and soaked the heel of my sock with blood, I kept on roguing. If you stuck to your job o' work, the squad stuck to you. After Big John's Dell, the front seat of the van belonged democratically to the two who got there first.

"Hey, Fredo!" said Bender. "Shut the window up a wee bit?"

Through the farm gate and up the brae to Crean was how most days started once we'd given the Morrisons' home crops their first roguing. When it came to their rented fields, the whole of Fife was our field of endeavour. Winding, sunken, Pictish roads bore us away each morning and brought us home again at evening to Wilma's kitchen table.

"Are you deaf in the front there?" shouted Bender. "I said shut it. You're raising up a desert storm in the back here. I'm trying to get some kip in."

The Bedford plunged into the gloom of the oak-leaf tunnel then dropped into second gear for the climb to the crest. There she lay across the water, shining in her morning glory – the fair city of Dundee. According to Kenny, most of the sandbags on the Western Front had been made in Dundee's jute factories. He kept his foot pressed down on the accelerator pedal to take advantage of the long downhill straight at Broomielaw. The Bedford's known top speed was 63 m.p.h., although both Tamas and Bender swore they had managed to get her up to 65 one day, when there had been no one else around to confirm it.

"Go on, Kenny old son. Go for it."

The red needle of the speedo showed 62 m.p.h. … 62 m.p.h …

"Go on, Kenny. Give it some welly."

63 m.p.h … 63 m.p.h. …

The Broomielaw gradient ran out as we approached the Biggery roundabout and the latest attempt on the record came to nothing, as it always did whenever there was someone else around. At Collessie we turned off the main road into the Howe of Fife, the rich vale of arable tilth that skirted the lower reaches of the high ground surmounted by the Twa Paps. That's when Bender realised where we were going.

"Kenny! Why in the holy name o' fuck did you let Davy rent out Kirkbuddo again this year?"

"Because Harry Blaine's a mate o' mine," said Kenny, "and mates stick together. If you had any mates o' your own you'd know that, Ben. Besides, Auld Andy himself has given Harry a good load o' new stock this year so all will be well."

"New stock? Christ, how many times have we heard that one before?"

A rutted track led to a stone steading built in an L-shape. There was no fancy new barn at Kirkbuddo. Its old hay mouldered under a rateaten tarpaulin. The farmhouse door opened and a sheep dog spurted out, followed by a stocky, white-haired gaffer with one shoulder strap of his dung-splattered dungarees hanging down.

"Kenny!" he called out. "Good to see you, sir!" Harry Blaine's dog led Shane off for a frolic.

"Draft all present and correct," said Kenny, saluting. "And yourself, young Harry?"

"Still here, am I no? Still standing."

Harry stood on his own ground and held out his arm to shepherd us indoors. A shotgun lay cocked open on his kitchen table. Our eyes slowly got used to the gloom. Harry fetched glasses and wiped them with a scrap of towel.

"The wean?" he said, nodding at Wee Eck.

"He's one o' us," confirmed Kenny, "for the purpose in hand."

Kirkbuddo was in sore need of a woman's touch. Nothing was clean or fresh. A cracked window pane had been patched with sticky tape.

"September the twenty-fifth!" said Harry, raising the first toast.

"Absent friends!"

"Old comrades!" answered Kenny.

Fredo and I sipped and swallowed.

"Scotland the Brave!" said Harry.

Bender, Tamas and Wee Eck raised their amber drams in unison.

"Scotland the Brave!!!"

Tamas and Bender were looking serious. Harry and Kenny were looking deadly serious. Wee Eck had tears in his eyes from the fire of the spirit. Another volley rang out.

"The Black Watch for ever!"

"The Fighting Fourth!"

Fredo and I kept our English mouths respectfully shut while the whisky scorched another runnel inside our gullets. Then we all set our empty glasses down and looked at them.

"And God rot the German Kaiser."

"Amen to that."

The buzz of a trapped fly intruded from another room.

"Right, lads," said Harry, getting down to business, "come away and I'll show you the field."

The dogs were waiting outside with their tongues hanging out.

"So long as it's not Dell you've got," said Tamas, "we'll be happy."

"No, no," said Harry, taking a half-smoked fag from behind his ear. "It's a new variety Auld Andy's given me this year. Honour. Supposed to be a good cropper. He said he'd paid twenty pound a ton for it."

"What did I tell you, lads?" said Kenny, rubbing his hands in anticipation. "Honour. Brand new and never been rogued before. This is our lucky day."

Harry Blaine's field of Honour was a bit like the man himself, stubborn of shape and very Fife-ish. He'd had to plough it cleverly, with a double endrig in one corner and a triple endrig diagonally opposite. Happily, his drills were flat and wide, so easy on the ankles, unlike the thrifty, narrow furrows we were used to on Morrison-ploughed land. Harry and Kenny chatted apart while the rest of us kitted-up at the back of the van. Fredo had found some old leather gardening gloves in the Lower Murtry summer house. He took the right-hand one and gave me the left.

"What's wrong, girls?" said Bender disgustedly. "Scared you'll chip your nail varnish?"

In fact, the gloves were an inspiration. With the season now well on, the blackleg was turning nasty. In its early stages blackleg showed up as a mere dark blush on the stem of the potato plant but by this stage of the season, liquefaction was beginning to set in. The technical term for a potato in the terminal stages of blackleg was 'minging'. Pulling out a plant that was minging with blackleg left your hand dripping with vegetable slime. Not that we were expecting any blackleg at Kirkbuddo. If Harry Blaine's crop of Honour really was pristine, it was the healthiest field of tatties we were likely to meet all season. We gathered round for a look-see.

"It reminds me a wee bit o' Arran," mused Kenny, folding over a stem with his stick to inspect the underside of the leaves.

Honour was a low grower with a tendency to sprawl. Its leaves were small with a hint of serration.

"Aye," said Harry dubiously, "except is it no a wee bit more leggy than the Arran?"

Harry's face was crinkled and veined, with patches of stubble where he hadn't shaved very well. A white scar accentuated the cleft between his tufty eyebrows. Kenny stooped suddenly and twisted a knot of lightly rooted leaves from the side of his drill.

"Groundies!"

We drifted a few yards up our drills to check for groundkeepers.

"Here's one." "And another." "Aw, shit a brick!"

Groundkeepers derived from potato scraps left in the ground after previous harvests. Any bit of old tattie was capable of taking root given an adequate supply of sun and water. In themselves, groundies were no worse than vagrant weeds but they counted as rogues to the Ministry of Agriculture's inspectors.

"Right, lads," said Kenny, putting on his brave face, "fall in. We'll do the endrig first to get the measure o' these groundies. Harry, I'll drop by later."

Harry whistled to his dog and Shane followed the pair of them as far as the gate.

"He has a fine eye on him," muttered Kenny, "if it's a sniper you need in a hurry. But when it comes to keeping his tatties in order … fucksake!"

Harry Blaine should never have put brand new, perfect seed in the same field he had used for tatties the year before.

"He was a sniper?" I said.

Before getting ten yards into the crop we were spotting groundies everywhere. Most were so weedy they came out with a kick.

"Yon Harry Blaine was as sharp as a pin," said Kenny, "until he got a taste o' his own medicine. Old Jerry set up a sniper against him and he clipped Harry's loophole one day and sent half a bullet into his puss. Our Harry was blinded in his right eye for nearly six months after that."

"Was he in your squad?"

"No lad. Bombers didn't mess wi' the snipers. Once you were in a squad, you stayed in it and hardly saw the rest o' the mob. Funny job, the sniping. You needed the temperament. Me and Billy were happy with the bombing until Loos. After that –"

At the endrig, we dumped our gleanings and Fredo surreptitiously removed his glove and I did the same. The time for gloves would come but not today.

"What a waste o' fine seed to stick it in here," sighed Kenny. The sun hammered down, high and hot. After the first round our sweaters came off; after the next our shirts. Bender's broad shoulders were softened by lard. Tamas's body looked as hard as white marble.

"Kenny," I said. "What happened at Loos? What actually happened to you there?"

He took off his flat cap and tucked it into his belt.

"Happened?" he said.

Kenny's shirt came off next. Above each elbow and around his neck was a sharp demarcation where his sun-browned skin ended and the white skin began. He turned his back.

"This is what happened to me at Loos, College –"

"Wow!" said Fredo.

It was a curved blue scar, about the size and shape of a sickle blade.

"Aw, please," grimaced Tamas. "Put it away Kenny. We've all seen it before."

The scar tissue was as thick as a welt. Kenny straightened his stoop as Fredo asked permission to prod him, out of professional curiosity.

"Did you lose any ribs?"

The scar began on the base of Kenny's neck and roughly followed the angle of his shoulder blade.

"Naw," said Kenny modestly, "it just bashed in a few o' them."

"It's occluded your *supra-spinatous fossa*," said Fredo, brazenly showing off his medical nous. "You're lucky you didn't lose the whole *coracoid*."

"But what happened?" I insisted.

"I've told you – the Battle o' Loos," said Kenny. "That's what happened. And this one –"

He showed us another scar, a clean white one above his left elbow.

"I said you'd set him off again," groaned Tamas. "Leave his carcase alone, for fucksake. One more round and it's piece break time. Christ, I hate Kirkbuddo."

Fredo rubbed in some of his sun cream and offered it round. "*Lotion!*" squawked Bender. "Christ, what kind o' poofy wee bastard do you take me for?"

The saft, wally English bastards were up to their usual tricks again. First gloves for the blackleg, now the lotion. The meaning of the Battle of Loos was forgotten.

"You'll be in agony tonight," said Fredo, "if you don't watch your back in this sun."

When Kenny accepted a dollop of lotion for the bald top of his head Bender pirouetted grotesquely in front of him.

"Oh Kenneth," he lisped. "You do thmell thweet."

Wee Eck held out his paws and took his medicine like a man. So did Tamas, surprisingly. His nose and the tops of his ears were already reddening from the sun. That Viking complexion of his needed taking care of.

"Jessies!" sneered Bender. "It's only the sun, for fucksake! That's all it is. Sun. I notice College here is no taking on any o' Fredo's lotion."

I stood there, shirt-less, brownest of the brown. Kenny caught on first, then the others. Sun lotion – for College!? Priceless! Fredo offered me the lotion.

"No thanks," I said. "I'm toasting nicely."

That was the precise moment that Fredo and I entered Murtry folklore. By the time Kenny had got over his coughing fit, 'No thanks,

I'm toasting nicely,' had made us immortal. Kenny called for the piece break there and then. We spread the spare sacks under the hospitable branches of a giant hornbeam and ate our pieces in the shade. Afterwards, Bender took the van to Collessie to re-stock on Irn Bru and Kenny and Shane went with him as far as the farm, for a blether over auld lang syne with Harry Blaine.

"And that's the last we'll see o' him today," predicted Tamas. "Bender's right. Davy should never have taken on Kirkbuddo. Yon Harry Blaine's a menace. Kenny is away to get pished again, like he did last year and the year before that."

"Leave him alone," said Fredo, mildly. "A wee dram does no one any harm at his age."

"Christ," said Tamas, "that auld cunt's got you two wrapped around his pinkie. I'll tell you one thing for sure – this is my last season at Murtry and that's a fact. Fuck it. Everyone's making top dollar at the roguing this year except us, stuck here, fucking about with a load o' fucking *groundies*!"

The van returned in a cloud of dust and Bender distributed the crisps and fizzy drinks. It was only afterwards, during the period usually reserved for Kenny's instructive reminiscences about potatoes, bombs, women and fishing, that we minded his absence.

"I told you," said Tamas, "he's down at the farm getting pished."

"Aye, we'll have to carry on without him," said Bender. "Come on, lads, there's a job o' work to be done remember."

It didn't feel quite right to me. Were we a properly constituted squad without Kenny? What was the drill? There had to be a Number Two to take over but – was it Bender? Wee Eck climbed obediently to his feet. Fredo and I weren't so sure. Neither of us two could be Number Two, obviously, on account of our racial inferiority, but what about –

"Relax," said Tamas, "ten more minutes won't do us any harm, Ben."

Tamas was too much of a selfish, bullying bastard to be Number Two. Wee Eck was too young. Fredo and I were too English. That left Bender. We rose groaningly and dragged ourselves into action.

"We are stupid, us lot," said Tamas. "That's what we are, plain stupid."

At three-thirty we finished the last round and Bender called a halt. Fredo and I were despatched to the farm to find out what had happened to Kenny.

"Check the back parlour," said Wee Eck. "That's where I found them last year."

Sure enough, there was Kenny, sprawled on the sofa, humming to himself, while Harry snored in his armchair with an extinct fag between his fingers. The room smelled hotly of cigarette smoke and whisky. They had emptied a bottle of 'Old Grouse' between them.

"Boys, my boys!" proclaimed Kenny, liltingly. "I knew I could count on you."

Outside, Bender sounded the Bedford's horn. I hooked Kenny under his armpits and Fredo took him by his boots. Wee Eck held open the doors.

"Stretcher bearers!' yelled Kenny. "At the double! Easy there. *Easy! I'm still alive, you saft wally bastards, very much so. 'Alive, alive-o-o! Alive, alive-o-o…' "

We laid Kenny in the back of the van, with a folded sack for a pillow.

"I'd put a gag on him if I was you," said Tamas. "Unless you want

'Mademoiselle from Armenteers' all the way home. He sings like a drain when he's pished."

Bender clapped the back doors shut and rattled the handle to make sure of the lock. At the crossroads, he shunned the main road and went straight over.

"That's the Frasers' place, over there," he said to Fredo in the front seat. "That'll be where you and Miss Jane will be getting your squashie in, if she ever asks you over for a game, which I somehow doubt, seeing as how you're a poofy English bastard who stinks o' poof's lotion all over."

Fredo yawned with commendable lack of interest. He knew all about the Frasers' place. Miss Jane had called for him at the Wank Hut two nights previously and whisked him off in one of her dad's Land Rovers. Afterwards, Fredo had sworn me to secrecy about the whole affair. It was none of the squad's business what he and Miss Jane got up to of an evening, the jammy, lotioned English bastard.

8 HAUNTED

The Ministry of Agriculture's Schedule of Potato Inspections (Scotland) for the year 1965 was a substantial document and was delivered to Lower Murtry with a comprehensive list of Ordnance Survey grid references for each field to be inspected. Davy held us roguers back for a tactical briefing after the morning muster in the yard. Kenny held the Schedule myopically close to his nose.

"Christ, it's your specs I'm needing, College," he sighed. "I can hardly read this at all."

Stern roguing was one thing, getting the rogued crops through their inspections required extra guile. Some of the Ministry's potato inspectors were failed roguers or ex-roguers, others were full-time supervisors. As such, they were known by name throughout the land.

"Aw Christ," said Bender, peering over Kenny's shoulder, "they're sending us Barry Mitchell, the bastards."

The Schedule of Inspections went from hand to hand until it was daubed with sticky dabs. One of the three inspectors assigned to the Morrison harvest was a woman, a previously unknown quantity by the name of Sheena Rattray.

"If you need someone to keep an eye on her," leered Tamas, "I'll keep her straight."

"It's yon Mitchell I'm worried about," said Davy. "He knocked down thirty-five acre o' Teds at Bankside for mild mosaic the year before last. He kens his tatties inside out, lads. You'll have to stick by him every step he takes. Like a leech."

"Aye but," said Kenny. "There's three o' them, Davy."

David Morrison's plans for the first-go inspections had only envisaged two inspectors. The addition of a supervisor would take away an extra roguer on escort duty. It was Murtry policy to shadow every inspector personally through every crop – to distract, argue and dissemble. Plus, there was another crisis of manpower. Wullie Sharp had gone absent without leave, last seen heading for New Buildings in the company of a berry picker half his age. Davy had no idea when Wullie might be back, if ever, and nor did his missus. In the meantime, someone else would have to drive the berry bus to Dundee and back.

"I'm your man for that job, Davy," said Tamas, quick as a flash. "Problem solved."

A whole day with Miss Jane and Big Lizzie at the berries! At that moment we hated Tamas more than ever.

"Bollocks to that!" said Bender. "This daft fuck will be in the ditch before he's half way up the brae. I'm your man for the bus, Davy. I know the route and everything."

"Tamas got there first," said Davy. "You boys have got a big job to do at Dunbog I'm told."

"Aye," said Kenny, "and we're late for it already, standing here blethering. Come on, boys. Let's get fell in."

Kenny folded the Schedule of Inspections and handed it back. Tamas sauntered off jangling the keys of the berry bus, licking his chops like a hungry fox.

* * * * *

Dunbog estate was a long drive in the Bedford to the other side of

Auchtermuchty. Bender sat in the front of the van with Wee Eck while Fredo and I sprawled in the back with Shane, trying to get some extra shut-eye. Fredo was knackered after his latest bout of squashie with Miss Jane. I was knackered from having to sit up half the night listening to him re-live the whole encounter in gloating detail.

"Come on, my sleeping beauties," said Kenny, unlocking the rear doors. "It's *jildi* time."

Dunbog's field of Teds seemed enormous. Its furthest reaches disappeared into the mist. But there was something solid and old fashioned in the King Edward that appealed to me. The Pentland family of potatoes personified a certain crisp modernity but the King Edward, with its whiskery leaves and upright, assertive style, came with a century of tradition behind it.

"Christ, they've mixed a ton o' spray round hereabouts," said Bender, wrinkling his nose.

Spilled chemical granules had stained the earth with evil blotches. A toxic reek thickened at the back of my throat. We were standing where yesterday's pesticide sprayer had stopped to replenish his tractor's tanks, round after round. Gas, boys, quick. An ecstasy of fumbling. We kitted up quickly and escaped to the far end of the field.

"Fuck this lot," grumped Bender, whacking the crop with his stick. "It's totally fucking minging. Look at it. We'll be here all fucking week."

A close look at the contents of the endrig suggested that the whole crop at Dunbog was riddled with leaf-roll. And what made it more galling was the thought of Tamas with Miss Jane.

"Aye, well," said Kenny, "we haven't got all week so keep your heads down and get stuck in. Hard pounding is the order of the day. The sooner it's done, the sooner it's done."

Hard, of course, was exactly how Kenny liked his pounding. From now on, with the first-go inspections almost upon us, every hour of daylight would be needed for roguing. The groundies in the Honour at Kirkbuddo, the Dell rogues in the Desiree at Wester Murtry and now these minging Teds at Dunbog – all three crops were clear-cut candidates for failure. We tramped each drill hauling out leaf-roll by the sack-load. Only Kenny seemed to be enjoying himself. The damper the weather, the more he coughed. The more he coughed, the more grateful he felt for a hard job o' work.

After the midday piece break, I wandered off to find a dry place. A track led through a wood to a deserted old steading with half the slates missing from its roof. A coping stone bore the carved date, 1888. What had once been some sort of kitchen garden was now a tangled jungle. The rhubarb in its derelict forcing frame had swollen to elephantine size. I plunged through gooseberry bushes into the remains of a once-elegant glasshouse.

'If you want a fuck, ring Parbroath 402 after 6pm.'

'I seen Sheila snogging Brian.'

'S.L. luvs B.T. for ever.'

In its sad state of ruin, the glasshouse spoke eloquently of the craftsmanship expended on its construction. Black, lagged heating pipes ran round the walls at knee height. I fiddled with a tarnished brass handle that had once opened a window frame.

'Rangers 3 – Celtic 0.'

The grapes had withered on the vine, and then the vine itself. No kitchen maid would come again with a basket for the peaches.

The only visitors these days were school kids, smokers of illicit fags, daubers on walls with spent match-sticks. I heard something and crouched low. Footsteps on glass. Was it one of the squad checking up on me? Or some half-crazed hermit with a shotgun? I wedged myself under fog-drenched leaves, heart pounding, but when I heard that distinctive cough I knew it wasn't the Hound of the Baskervilles or the Auchtermuchty Ripper.

"Kenny!"

He span round with his roguing stick at the ready.

"College! Christ! You fucking near scared me out o' my fucking wits!"

"Sorry," I said. "I was pretty spooked myself."

"Spooked?" said Kenny. "You near enough gave me a fucking heart attack What are you doing here anyway, looking for a dry place to shite in?"

The extensive park around Dunbog House had been rented out and ploughed under. Some of the original trees remained in noble isolation, hooped in Victorian iron. Round one corner of the big house was an artificial lake clogged with fallen branches.

"Aha!" said Kenny, probing under the bushes with the point of his roguing stick. "Come here, you wee beauty."

He bent down on one knee and fished out his clasp knife. He had found a shy little plant with bright blue flowers.

"For the missus, like," he said.

He sliced a pot-sized divot from around the plant and wheedled it out. By missus he meant Auld Andy's wife, Queanie Morrison, a known fanatical gardener. Kenny fitted the rooted clump of earth into his jacket pocket and cupped its weight in the palm of his hand.

"In the old days afore the war," he said, "there used to be a fair sized rockery hereabouts. Mrs Fyvie used to buy plants from all the catalogues and get them sent here. It was a beautiful place, Dunbog, fifty years ago. The Fyvie's were famous for it."

Kenny turned to face the big house. The Victorians had rather spoiled its Palladian symmetry by connecting it to the coach house and steading of the home farm. The roof had long gone. Mighty brick chimneys reared up, un-buttressed. The windows were full of bleak mist.

"The lawyers took the roof off," said Kenny, "to save money on the rates."

We skirted the stagnant lake and climbed a tumulus riddled with rabbit holes. The monument on top was a broken pillar on a plinth.

'To the eternal memory of Donald McIver Alwyn Fyvie, killed in action, Ypres, November 24th, 1914, aged 22 years, also of Iain McIver Alwyn Fyvie, missing in action, Le Transloy, September 30th, 1916, aged 19 years.'

"It finished her off," said Kenny, "losing both her boys like that. She drew the blinds and never smiled again. I used to work up here sometimes, after the war, at the harvesting, but I never once saw her, not once. She let her factor run the place, Budgie Bingham. Yet she lived on long enough. The Widow Fyvie was ninety year old when she croaked. The whole lot's ended up with some nephew in Canada who's never yet come near the place." Kenny's war cast its long shadow.

"Where's Le Transloy?" I asked.

"No idea," said Kenny, looking into the mist.

"Did you ever go to Ypres, Kenny?"

"It was called Eeps," he said. "The Salient. We didn't call it Eeprez.

Of course I was there. What else do you think I've been blethering about all these days? Everyone in the British Army ended up in the Salient if he lived long enough. First there was Neuve Chapelle, for a practice like, then there was Loos in 1915, then there was the Somme, in 1916, which I missed because o' my shoulder, and then there was the Salient, 1917. Paschendaele, they called it. Christ, you knew you were in the war when you got to the Salient. We thought it would never end."

He stamped down the grass and nettles obscuring the Fyvie boys' memorial. Snail trails had besmirched the carved inscription.

'Two brothers, one destiny.'

Kenny wiped away the dirt of encrustation until the message was visible once again.

"Are Donald and Iain buried here?"

"No son," said Kenny. "No one's buried here. It was against the rules. Wherever you copped it in France, that's where you stayed."

"So the Fyvies are still out there?"

"The Fyvies are still out there," confirmed Kenny. "Our Billy's still out there. They're all still out there, College."

The Great War had emptied Fife of its finest.

"And the Muzzie-boys? They're still out there?"

"All o' them," confirmed Kenny. "Muzzie-boys. Aussie-boys. Canucks. The whole lot. Everybody. Frogs and Krauts. Millions o' them. Yanks. Eyeties. New Zealanders. Chinks. They're all still out there, millions upon millions."

A nearby crow called to his brother crow. They were the first birds I had heard all day.

" 'Look down', " I said, "' and swear by the slain of the War that you'll never forget – '."

"Forget?" said Kenny. "How could anyone forget? There's hardly a day goes by when I don't think o' Billy Rankin. You can never forget your squad, College. Not if you've been through a battle wi' them."

The bright blue flowers peeped from his pocket. The crows, wherever they were, stayed silent.

"Let's away then," said Kenny at last, reaching for a corner of the Widow Fyvie's plinth by which to haul himself up.

"I'll catch you later," I said, ducking aside.

"Well don't be long at it. There's a big job to be done here, College. Christ knows but this is turning into a hard season."

The front door of Dunbog House had been kicked off its hinges. A grand staircase, with random banisters missing, led up to a square of grey sky. The mantel piece in the dining room had been wrenched out, leaving a hole of smoke-blackened brick to mark where the proud, brave Fyvies had once gathered round the family hearth. I found a dry corner to squat in then left in a hurry.

* * * * *

We finished the Teds at Dunbog in near silence. The fog did not lift all day but seeped into every crevice, dampening our spirits. We communicated in grunts and took our fag breaks like beasts, wordlessly, under the dripping trees. The drab mood only began to lighten on the way home when we stopped at New Buildings to re-supply at Hastie's Hardware & General Merchants. Mr and Mrs Hastie ran the kind of licensed store that stayed open all hours for any known and valued customer who might be looking for a zinc bucket in a hurry, or a packet of turnip seed. I bought myself a new diary, an exercise book of 32 pages with the multiplication tables conveniently displayed on the back cover. Mrs Hastie was also able to supply me with a picture postcard for Grandad and my mother in Lichfield.

"Fucksake," sneered Bender, "has your mammy never seen a Scottie dog before?"

"The alternative," I explained, "was some saft wally Scotch bastard playing the bagpipes with a sprig of heather up his arse."

"Don't you put the mockers on the pipes, sir," scolded Kenny. "They lifted us more than once, out in France. Christ, you English don't know the half o' it. It's the best laxative in the world when His Majesty's enemies hear yon pipes a-coming over."

When we got back to Lower Murtry, Fredo spent a long time in the bathroom and was first to finish the goulash that Wilma had left out for us on the hob. Back at the Wank Hut Miss Jane was waiting, sitting in her daddy's Land Rover with two squash racquets on the seat beside her. She had parked round the back so she couldn't be seen from the road. Fredo made a pathetic attempt at looking surprised.

"Oh!" he said. "Jane! Hi! What a pleasant surprise!"

He changed into his plimsolls and they were off, the pair of them, with eyes only for each other, leaving me with the Sputniki for company. I made a cup of tea with the makings I'd bought at Hastie's and tackled my new diary.

'Sunday, August 4th. Fog most of the day. 25 acres Teds at Dunbog – a spooky old house in a rather fine Georgian park. Fredo is definitely a jammy bastard. He's gone off to play squash with the Goddess for the second time this week. Race riots in Los Angeles.'

9 INSPECTORS

The morning of the first inspections dawned with a thin mist rising along the shore of the silvery Tay. The patriarch himself, Auld Andy, stood by his youngest son's shoulder as the men of Murtry mustered in the yard. As well as the tattie roguing, the berry picking was entering its most intense phase. This was the climax of the growing season. Any strawbs or rasps that weren't harvested in the next few days would be fit only for Dundee's jam factories. It was time for maximum effort all round.

"We're looking for a good year, this year," urged Auld Andy. "We're counting on you, lads. So –"

There was a pause, an air of expectation. We stood ready to do or die for common good. Every pair of eyes was fixed on Auld Andy.

"So – do your best, eh?"

That marked the limit of his exhortatory powers. 'Do your best, eh?' His men shuffled their dusty feet.

"Aye aye, Andy."

It was left to Kenny to step into the rhetorical breach.

"Well you've good enough men for it," he declared. "We've been at it like Trojans at the tatties, that's for sure."

Auld Andy's white shirt left no doubt which of the two men had a woman at home to help him dress to impress. Andy Morrison was a boss from the tip of his polished toe caps to the top of his Brylcreemed head. He had built solidly and begat sons in his likeness. Men like Andy Morrison had been put on this earth to take the chances that came their way and suffer righteous increase in the sight of the Lord. Kenny Roberts was the one you would follow if your life depended on it.

"We'll see how they want to play it," said Davy, after the orramen had peeled off, "but I'm thinking of putting College and Fredo wi' the inspectors today. Dad and me will take Mad Mitch."

"Aye," said Kenny. "That should keep him quiet. And you two boys, you're fit for it?"

Fredo and I nodded seriously. What had seemed mere weeks ago to be a vastly complicated body of potato lore had resolved itself into a hard core of knowledge. You had to know what you were looking for. You had to stay in the game. Whatever happened, you had to finish the job.

"If they find anything they're not damned sure about, young Woggie," said Auld Andy, "don't be feared to argue the toss. Use any old blethers you want, son, just keep them distracted. Understand?"

"Aye," said Davy. "Distraction. That's the name o' the game. Distract them every way you can."

"And while you're at it, young Woggie," said Tamas, "remember to keep your hands off o' yon Sheena in case I fancy a shunt at it myself, if I gets half a chance."

Kenny and the lads rattled off in the Bedford, leaving Fredo and me to work planks off the sawmill until the inspectors arrived. Mad Mitch seemed perfectly affable, brisk not deferential. Auld Andy was up to his tricks immediately, fussing around the doors of the inspectors' car, interfering in the unfolding of their maps.

"He's a bit up himself, your gaffer," said Sheena, watching the

Morrisons and Mad Mitch zoom off in Auld Andy's Jag.

She had wasted no time latching on to Fredo.

"Oh, the old man's not so bad," he said. "What do you fancy inspecting first, the Dell or the Crown? They're both in good nick"

Sheena consulted her Schedule and decided it would be sensible to start at the furthest point and work back to the big house in time for lunch. Miss Jane waved cheerfully as we skirted the bottom of the berry field. We did not tarry. If any crop was going to fail its first go it would surely be Big John's Desiree-infested Dell. Distraction was the name of the game.

"Have you come far?" I said.

"Nah. Only from Cupar."

My inspector seemed resolute in his refusal to be distracted. I knew his type. St. Andrews was full of hard-working young Scots determined to make their way in the world.

"What are your digs like?" I said, distractingly.

"So-so."

My English accent, if nothing else about me, had put him instantly on the defensive.

"What did she give you for breakfast?"

Distraction. Distraction. My inspector made eye contact for the first time, witheringly.

"Porridge and toast," he said. "Thank you for asking."

When we got to the Dell, the inspectors paced off ten yards each to select the drills they would inspect. My inspector had hardly gone more than twenty yards into his drill when I spotted the first leaf-roll looming. It was a big one. Even the leaves on top had started to turn yellow. My mind went blank. It was inconceivable that he could miss it. He missed it. Perhaps he was walking too fast. Or maybe it was too early in the season for him to yet have his eye in. He reached the end of his drill with nothing to show but a clear conscience. Sheena dropped something at his feet.

"Leaf-roll."

She seemed pleased with herself. Fredo joined us.

"Actually, we didn't find much leaf-roll in this crop at all," he said perplexedly.

I scratched my head.

"Nope. It was pretty clean as I recall." "We did get *some* leaf-roll."

"Not much."

"Hardly any."

"Nothing serious."

"That," said Sheena, pointing her Ministry of Agriculture walking stick with the air of a hardened pro, "is a definite leaf-roll. I'm going to have to mark it."

Fredo and I stood apart while the inspectors muttered to themselves, marking up their forms.

"Mine missed an absolute minger," I said.

"Mine missed a Desiree," said Fredo, "in full bloom."

The two inspectors sampled six drills of Big John's Dell and between them chalked up a bare handful of black marks. Sheena had got her eye in on leaf-rolls and added a couple more to her tally. Her colleague, feeling under pressure to find *something* incriminating, identified an alleged case of mild mosaic and put a sample into a plastic bag for analysis at the Ministry of Agriculture's laboratory.

"So that crop's passed has it?" said Fredo.

"We've seen worse," said Sheena. "We've had failures already. But if that one does turn out to be Mild we'll be back."

A single specimen of Mild Mosaic in a crop of twenty-odd acres was nothing to worry about, especially since – as we had emphatically pointed out – it was fake Mild, the result of spray damage. Somehow, Big John's minging, Desiree-riddled Pentland Dell had passed its first-go.

"Hot isn't it," said Sheena, pulling her woolly jumper over her head. "Tatties is hard work alright."

We dawdled back through the strawberries, picking a few on the way. Miss Jane came over to see how her father's crop had fared, which allowed Fredo to bask in the glow of her approbation.

"Here," she said, "help yourself. Take a punnet. Plenty to spare."

The inspectors filled a plump punnet each of ripe, juicy strawberries. We had all the time in the world to tarry, now that the inspectors had got it into their heads that Murtry was a generous place endowed with fine, healthy crops. Big John's second field of Dell passed as easily as the first. Likewise, the Majestics at neighbouring Kilspindle. Accordingly, lunch at the big house was a jolly affair. When Davy came back with Mad Mitch – having secured clean sheets from the inspections at Pittendrie, Lenzie and Balverdie Mains – he gave me and Fredo the rest of the day off.

"Those inspectors are rubbish," said Fredo, as we stood outside the kitchen door waving them off to their next farm. "All they could think about was finishing early."

"We'll see if they're rubbish or no," said Davy, "when they come back for the next lot. That Mitchell boy's no fool. He's getting his eye in sure enough."

The inspectors would be back the next day, and the day after that, until every Morrison crop had been certified. That was the law of the land. Only when every field had passed its first-go *and* its second would the squad of '65 have passed the Murtry test. As soon as tea was finished, Fredo scooted off to his goddess leaving me to the delights of the cricket news in 'The Daily Telegraph' that Mad Mitch had left behind. A sudden spurt of form from Glamorgan had put them in contention for the County Championship. Only if D'Oliveira and the boys won every remaining match would Worcestershire retain their title. I was sitting at the Wank Hut's kitchen table, when there was a cough at the open door. It was Kenny, dropping by with his shotgun.

"I'm thinking o' heading up Crean way," he said, "to see what's what."

Fredo got the girl, I got the country walk with the old geezer. Kenny led the way across the lane and up into the wood, stopping briefly at the quarry to poke a fresh turd with his boot.

"The old fox is back," he decided.

Two white scuts flashed in the greenery and disappeared. Whatever Kenny was after with his gun, it wasn't rabbits at close range. At the crest of the ridge we rested against smooth Druidic boulders to let the day's store of trapped heat seep into us. Generations of farmboys had tarried at the crest of Crean Law to see what was what. The Lower Murtry big house lay under direct observation. Down in the paddock, someone was marching purposefully in wide circles, stopping every now and then to whirl something above his head. It was Bender, practising his hammer throwing.

"He's getting himself fit for the weekend," said Kenny. "It's a bad day for our Ben when he doesn't come back from the Highland Games wi' a tenner to show for it."

Bender had a pair of special boots with metal plates nailed to them, for extra grip in the tug o' war. He was also a fair hand at tossing the caber but the hammer was his main event. He had won medals for it all over Scotland. Kenny pointed to the horizon with a chewed grass stem.

"Sometimes," he said, "when I'm up here of a nice, clear summer's eve, I can sometimes spy Schiehallion over yonder. If the light catches her right. That's more than thirty miles away."

I focused on the far distant line of blue mountains.

"That's where Pontius Pilate was born," said Kenny, "over in Perthshire somewheres."

I cleaned my specs with the hem of my shirt.

"Pontius Pilate? The one in the Bible?"

"Aye, lad. The Royal Scots – Pontius Pilate's bodyguard. Oldest regiment in the world. First o' Foot and Right o' the Line."

Westward I spied the chimneys and slate roofs of New Buildings. Its kirk spire and the chimney by the railway yard stood out clearly. Even through clean lenses I could not see the peak of Schiehallion.

"Aye," said Kenny complacently, "you've to know what you're looking for, right enough."

Downhill, Kenny paused on the other side of the burn to investigate some deer tracks. In Crean's old kirkyard the daisies growing in the shadow of the stone dyke had closed early for sleep. I peered through a side window. Dust had settled thickly.

"We all used to kirk here when Auld Gillespie had the living of it," remembered Kenny. "They shut it down for good when he died. We've been lumped in wi' the Dalbeattie lot ever since, except for funerals. We still plant folk here when they're done for, from time to time."

Crean marked the border between the world of Murtry and the rest of the known universe. Here, by the gatepost of the ruined smithy, was the trodden patch of grass where car-less folk waited for the bus to come along. I pushed aside a giant hogweed and crossed a hidden threshold.

"He was well crafty," said Kenny, "when it came to fixing tackle. Folk used to come from Dairsie and Dalry and all over to have Billy's dad fix their gear for them."

Square holes in the stone gables showed where rafters had been extracted for use elsewhere.

"We had some braw times before the war, me and Billy."

I saw the two of them in the postcard Kenny had showed me, posing in their kilts against that preposterous simulacrum of a Flemish rose bower. Crean smithy spoke of everything I needed to know about Kenny and his war. Behind its roofless walls was a garden smothered in bean plants. Kenny howked around with the heel of his boot and uncovered what looked like a small gravestone.

"They're not buried here?" I said. "Are they?"

"Don't be daft," said Kenny. "Danny Rankin's buried in yon kirkyard. And his missus."

"So who's under this?"

"It's Billy's motorbike."

The Rankins had lost their Billy to the war in 1915. Denied his body they'd buried his bike.

"It was a Carlton Phoenix," said Kenny. "Three-and-a-half horse power. The Earl's cousins, the Stewart-Farqharsons, had Dalbeattie House that summer. The Phoenix belonged to one o' their boys. The first we knew about it was the racket it made. Me and Billy got out o' Sconsie Wood just in time to see the young Honourable What's-His-Face whooshing up the brae with his arse in the air, hanging on for dear life. When our Billy saw that motorbike –"

Kenny's voice thickened at the memory so that he had to cough out the rest.

"Well, one look at it, College, and our Billy was *hooked*."

Deep among the bean leaves a blackbird had begun to argue with itself. Kenny handed me his tin of tobacco makings. Every time I had ever tried to roll a cigarette I'd made a hash of it.

"A few days afterwards," Kenny resumed, "the Dalbeattie factor, Frank Leishman, was up here at the smiddy wi' that same Phoenix. Its front wheel was buckled and its forks all bent to fuck. 'Don't bother fixing it, Danny,' he says, 'you've just to pretend. The young maister's cowped it into a ditch and bust his nose and his Ma wants it out o' the way till they're all off home again.' Danny Rankin got half a sov for keeping that Phoenix under wraps and afterwards Billy got it for keeps and fixed it up."

Kenny's cigarette pencilled a grey line of smoke against the hush. I picked up his shotgun to aim at nothing in particular. I felt its steely disapproval so set it down quick the way I'd found it.

"Billy's Ma went demented when she got the telegram he was dead. She took a hammer to all his things and smashed the lot. Table, chest, chair, fishing rod. Smashed them to pieces. Burnt his clothes. What was the point?"

"Where is he buried?"

"Our Billy's no buried."

The blackbird stopped its yellow beak. Kenny made the slightest of nods to the East. The lads were never coming back. "What happened?"

Kenny's gizzard swallowed emptily.

"The Battle of Loos, son. That's what happened."

Billy Rankin had shared his fags with Kenny Roberts and bought him drinks in the Old Brig Tavern. In this garden, they had heard the blackbird's song, followed by silence. What had happened to them out in France, in 1915, was not a difficult thing to talk about, it was an impossible thing.

"How did he die?"

"He didn't die," said Kenny. "He was killed. There's a difference."

"Were you there?"

"I was."

Some copped it, some went missing. Those lost were ordained never to be found.

"So what happened?"

"I don't know exactly."

"Didn't you see?"

Suddenly, Kenny's gun was where it belonged. I saw a blur and felt the blast. On the other side of the garden wall was a cornfield with half its crop gathered in and the lines of stubble showing clean and sharp in its endrig. Something hit the ground without a bounce, like a thrown cushion. A few feathers fluttered in mid-air like cartoon feathers.

"Good shot."

Kenny's ejected cartridge steamed on the grave of Billy Rankin's motorbike.

"Every shot's a good shot if you're ready for it."

No second target presented itself. After a minute or so Kenny leaned his gun aside and went to retrieve his prey. It was typical of Shane to be nowhere around when he was needed. Kenny stuffed the bird in his bag and rested his bent back against the garden wall, watching the horizon.

"The thing is," he said, "Loos was a proper battle, total mayhem, indescribable. That's the thing about a battle, you can't understand it. The whistle blows and off you go. You keep your head down. You follow orders. It's your training that gets you through. Otherwise it's just mayhem and murder and a million different things all going wrong at once."

Kenny re-lit the end of his cigarette with squinting concentration.

"If you could get any o' that there Indi-jabber translated for me," he said, "that might be a start to finding out what happened."

I had forgotten about the scrip he'd given me. It seemed rather late, after fifty years, for Kenny to be making a start on deciphering the Battle of Loos.

"I'll see my mum about it," I said. "I'll do my best."

"Aye. That's right, son. That's good enough for me."

"You should go back, Kenny, to France, before it's too late. Take a look-see. After the harvest."

For fifty years he had been wondering and waiting and always remembering Our Billy. None if it had been forgotten, it was all locked inside him still.

"Aye," he said. "Mebbe you're right."

"France," I said. "Eeps. You should go back. For a look-see. After the harvest and before winter sets in. You might find something."

"Mebbe," he said. "It's all still out there, that's for sure."

I carried Kenny's gun as far as the Wank Hut, by which stage it had begun to impress a bruise on my shoulder. We stood by the gate watching the last swifts skim the insect haze above the berry field. High in the Western sky the last of the day flared to its pink and orange crescendo.

"If I were to go," said Kenny, "would you mind coming wi' me, young College? I could use them pomes and quotes o' yours out there. If you're up for it, like."

Billy and the Fyvies were out there. The Punjabis and the Canucks were out there. I could see how poems and quotes might be useful to anyone seeking to re-fight the Battle of Loos after fifty years of thinking about it. But Fredo and I had made other plans. We were going to see the great cities of Europe by Inter-Rail. It had all been planned.

"Aye, well," said Kenny. "If you should change your mind like, in the meantime ..."

We tarried a while longer, admiring the sunset. Kenny smoked off the last of the fag he had tucked behind his ear and hoisted his hype with a grunt.

"Oh, and by the way," he said, "the next time you carry this thing for me I'd be grateful if you'd put the safety catch on. I've seen some nasty accidents happen the way you were doing it."

10 THE CEILIDH

Day after day, field after field, round after round, the roguing brought Fredo and me to the peak of physical hardness. We *powered* through those last inspections of the 1965 tattie season. The Ministry's inspectors were no match for the best squad in Fife bar none. Hector's five fields at Pittendrie Top passed their FS grade no problem, so did the Dunbog Teds. The Piper at Howieson's, the Javelin at Stuart Stanley's, the Standard at the Murchisons' and the Desiree at Balverdie all passed with flying colours. The last crop remaining was Harry Blaine's Honour.

"Kenny, relax for fucksake," said Bender. "There's nothing but groundies to worry about."

We were at our piece break, having pulled out barely half a sack from Kirkbuddo all morning. The Honour was as clean as ever, apart from the groundkeepers. But those few alien sprigs could get it failed as surely as half a ton of blackleg. A random thought crossed Bender's mind and found utterance.

"Are you bringing Muriel to the hop on Saturday?"

"Sure I'm bringing Muriel to the hop on Saturday," replied Tamas. "Who else would I be bringing, the Queen o' fucking Sheba?"

It was a Murtry tradition to celebrate a good year's harvest with a *ceilidh*. Already, the word had spread that the Morrisons were heading for a bumper yield, financially speaking.

"How about yourself, College?" said Tamas. "Should I get Muriel to bring along a couple o' Gunnie lassies, for you and Fredo at the *ceilidh*?"

Harry Blaine's Honour was the last field of the season. This was our very last piece break.

"Yes please," I said, automatically. "Something with nice big jugs on the front o' it."

This was our last day as a squad.

"How about you, Fredo?" said Tamas. "Fancy a wee bit o' something on Saturday night wi' nice big jugs on the front o' it?"

I had been happy these past few weeks, day after day, field after field, living in the moment, adrift from the past, without care of the future, day after day with my squad.

"Thanks Tamas," said Fredo. "That's a very kind offer. But I've made my own arrangements for Saturday night. I'll be shunting the Queen o' Sheba as usual."

Victory or dishonour. In the field alongside us, Harry Blaine's orraman was gathering in the yellow wheat in a combine harvester. A green John Deere tractor with Harry in the cab pulled away from the combine with a trailer full of grain. Kenny sucked on his stained front teeth, a sure sign that he was about to impart wisdom.

"You boys," he said, "are but ignorant loons when it comes to women. They've all got jugs on them. But can they make a broth from a shin bone? Eh? That's the question you need to be asking – is your woman handy about the place? Now, *raus* yourselves and let's see some *jildi* one more time. Half-a-dozen rounds and we're finished for the year."

I examined the wispy groundies that constituted our pile of shaws. They looked innocent enough. They could have failed the whole crop.

"We need to rogue this whole field again," I announced.

Being finished for the year was suddenly the last thing I wanted.

"College!" squawked Bender. "Have you gone stark, raving bampot or what?"

"Give him some lotion quick," said Tamas. "The sun's sent him hysterical."

"Happen he's right, lads," said Kenny. "There's too much in it yet. Fair's fair. We owe it to auld Harry."

I had spoken what was on his mind. There were still too many groundies in the Honour, it was as simple as that. Tamas bellowed with rage.

"Owe what to Harry, for fucksake? What about what Harry owes us?"

Fredo stood up and fell into line.

"They're right, lads," he said, "about the groundies. There's too many o' them yet. One more go should see it right."

"Those fucking inspectors are shite!" said Tamas. "They'll pass anything. They passed Big John's minging Dell, for fucksake."

Wee Eck stopped his whittling and fell into line, saying nothing in that impressive way of his.

"Fine," said Tamas. "If that's the way you lot want to play it – fine. But you lot can all fuck off and do it yourselves. We're no budging."

The four of us left Bender and Tamas under the hornbeam and fucked off to do it ourselves. Bender joined in at the end of the first round, Tamas at the end of the second. They had no choice. We were a squad.

* * * * *

The next day the supervisor, Barry Mitchell, signed and stamped the last of the Ministry of Agriculture's certificates and Davy stashed them in the Lower Murtry safe, treasure in the bank. For the rest of the day we helped out in the new barn, sweeping and swabbing, setting things up for the *ceilidh*. Wee Eck shimmied up like a monkey and hung the high girders with coloured light bulbs. Wilma and her sisters spread a feast on the same trestle tables that had been used for the weighing and paying of the berries – smoked hams, chickens roasted in the honey from Wilma's bees' plus bowls of potato mayonnaise and heaped helpings of fresh salads from the hothouse. There were a couple of poached salmon too, including one with dented head that I thought I recognised. That night, Fredo and I changed into our English clothes for the first time in weeks.

"I say, boys, but you're both looking gallus the night," said Queanie Morrison, twinkling flirtatiously as she heaped calories onto our paper plates. "If I was forty years younger …"

Bender steered us to the bar where Auld Andy and his three sons were handing out drinks as fast as they could pour them. It was most definitely not a night for the stinting of Murtry hospitality. Crowds of beefy Fifers stood around drinking and smoking while their womenfolk nibbled cheesy niblets and chatted among themselves on the straw bales set aside to create a fire hazard.

"A couple o' large jars for the English bastards if you don't mind!" demanded Bender.

Old Man Howieson raised his glass in our direction and Cyril Henderson's lads raised theirs.

"Aye-aye! Here's to the English bastards!"

A surge of boozy bonhomie drew us into the male embrace. All through the season our fame had spread. People wanted to shake hands with the wog and the wop the Morrisons had taken on.

"Stick it there, pal."

"How you doing, sir?"

"Need a wee top-up?"

"Watch out boys, the poofs have arrived."

It was Tamas. He slapped us on the back and offered cigarettes.

"Muriel," he said, "I want you to meet them saft, wally English bastards that I think I may have mentioned once or twice – College and Fredo."

Muriel, Princess of Gunnie, offered us each her hand in turn. She was bright eyed and plumptiously jugged in front, eminently shuntable in other words.

"*Enchante*," said Fredo, raising her scarlet finger-nails to his lips. "Muriel, you're completely wasted on that lummox, Tamas. Will you run away with me?"

"See what I mean?" beamed Tamas. "What a pair. Fucking English poofs all over."

Behind us, on a low-loader trailer pressed into duty as a stage, the band was tuning up. The Nicky Tams had come all the way from Auchtermuchty in a Bedford van just like our own.

"You'll be limbering up for a wee birl then, boys?" insinuated a voice behind us.

"Kenny! Come here, you old rascal!"

It was Kenny alright, in dapper disguise. He ran a nicotined finger round the inside of his white collar. In his regimental tie and tweed jacket he looked exactly like an old sodger out on the spree. A loud chord from the Nicky Tams cut through the barn's ambient buzz.

Someone gripped my upper arm and it turned out to be Big Lizzie Purdom in a long tartan skirt with a matching sash across her buxom. She pushed me towards the dance floor.

"Excuse me," I said, "I thought it was the man who took the lead?"

"This is Fife, remember. We're forward kind o' folk."

The first dance was 'Strip the Willow'. I had come across it at St. Andrews. After a faltering start my feet soon worked out where to go. Big Lizzie was graceful not gallumphing. Fredo and Miss Jane birled passed, then Kenny with Wilma in his arms.

"You've done this before," said Big Lizzie. "I'm glad you're not a total embarrassment."

"Thanks," I said. "I think it's the drink."

After the first dance Big Lizzie kept hold of my hot hand to make sure of the second. The Nicky Tams paused only for the quickest of adjustments at the end of each number before plunging into the next. If you didn't know the steps, you made them up. The inspector, Sheena Rattray, and Bender bumped into us, laughing their heads off. I danced with Miss Jane and Wee Eck's mum, and then danced a foursome with Queanie Morrison and Old Man Howieson's missus that left me gasping in pain due to a stitch in my side. Big Lizzie was the best dancer of the lot for a beginner like me. By half time we had sealed some kind of pact, or rather our raging hormones had.

Auld Andy mounted the stage and cleared his throat into the microphone for another of his terse extemporisations. Kenny replied with a toast to the Morrisons' hospitality that awarded special mention to Wilma and her sisters for the feast they had prepared, which everyone applauded long and loud, which brought a sweet smile to Wilma's face but only briefly. Davy Morrison climbed up to toast us roguers and our clean sheet, to which Bender made reply. Big John Morrison toasted the berry-pickers, to which the radiant Miss Jane replied. The comic turn of the night was provided by Tamas, who – having sunk his six pints – tried to propose a toast to Elvis Presley but missed his footing as he climbed onstage and had to be taken in hand by the Princess, at which point the Nicky Tams blasted back into action with a riproarious 'Dashing White Sergeant'. The night's programme ended with 'Auld Lang Syne' after which Auld Andy and Queanie stood in the yard for the final farewells.

"Fancy some night air?" said Big Lizzie.

Stacked high around the portable sawmill were the empty crates that would be used in a couple of months for shipping Murtry's tatties down south. Big Lizzie nudged me into a chimney of darkness between rough, resin-scented planks.

"What's wrong?" she said. "You're very quiet. Cat got your tongue?"

Sex had got my tongue.

"You feel hot," was the best I could manage.

We kissed with clumsy urgency, like amateurs, until the tip of her tongue found mine and the news flashed urgently to my brain: *she's ganting for it!* I fumbled at the top button of her blouse and realised that she was feeling for me at the same time. Her nipples puckered like juicy raisins. She breathed into my ear and the next thing I knew her blouse was open.

"Not here," she grunted thickly. "Not in the yard."

Big Lizzie steadied herself at the knees. The topmost of the stacked crates teetered against the starry sky. A wild thought seized me: why not here? For what other purpose were farmyards intended? Big Lizzie's skirt was buttoned up like some Highland Granny's. I fiddled hopefully at the waistband.

"*Shhh!*"

Two whisperers in the dark passed within inches, male and female, of whom I caught only a hint of Shalimar perfume and the glimpse of a tweed shoulder. On tip toe, clinging to the shadows, we crept towards the summer house like burglars. Big Lizzie blew out the match I lit.

"For God's sake! Do you want the whole o' Murtry down here for the show?"

The matchstick smouldered sulphrously in the warm dark. Big Lizzie stooped to kick off her shoes, revealing through her unbuttoned blouse the jugs I wanted so urgently to adore.

"Are you going to stand there all night, gawping?"

She hitched at something and her skirt fell to the floor. Her legs were straight and strong like a statue's.

"Your skin looks blue," she said.

"It's the moonlight," I mumbled, stupid with lust.

She stepped into my arms. Her muscles felt sleek and hard. We kissed properly. She unzipped me and wriggled her hand inside.

"You've done this before," I said.

My words came out in thick, coagulated lumps.

"*Ouch!*"

I was as stiff as a broom handle.

"Sorry," she said.

I concentrated on the mechanics, heading into unknown territory. Big Lizzie dragged me down onto the dusty cushions. I was going all the way this time. This was my night. This was my night of nights. I wanted witnesses. Where was my squad, for fucksake?

Look at me, lads. Look. College is doing it. COLLEGE IS DOING IT!

"This is your first time, isn't it?" said Big Lizzie.

The planks grazed my knees as I she guided me in.

"Not at all. What makes you think that?"

She gasped hotly into my ear. The joists of the summer house rocked creakily beneath us. I felt something stuck to the skin of her back – the butt end of a thinly rolled cigarette.

"What was that?" she said, as I flicked it away.

In my mind's eye I saw a fragment of the night I had just lived through, the potato crates, the back of an old sodger with his arm round a thin woman's waist.

"Nothing," I said. "I think I love you."

* * * * *

The morning after the ceilidh was the first day for weeks that we roguers didn't have to wake at six thirty a.m. for a hard day in the fields. My head felt surprisingly clear when I woke at six thirty, regardless. Outside, sparrows chirped in their dust-bath by the Wank Hut's front step. Fredo's sleeping bag was empty. He must have stayed out all night like a fox on the prowl. My roguing jeans stood upright in the corner, empty and bow-legged, as stiff as board from all the dried sap and potato starch they had absorbed, layer upon layer, day after day, week after week. I dressed in last night's English clothes again and opened the kitchen door. My manhood had begun. Thank you, Big Lizzie. Thank you. Thank you.

I slapped a few rashers in the black frying pan and sawed a slice off the loaf. Sure enough the next thing I heard was the Wester Murtry Land Rover cresting the brae. Fredo's eyes were red, his hair a mess.

"Are you so hungry," I asked, "you could eat a whole danged hoss?"

'Bonanza' was our favourite telly programme. Those Cartwright brothers sure knew how to live – riding the range, rounding up steers, shooting rustlers whenever the need arose.

"Yes'm," said Fredo. "It sure would do me some good to get outside o' them thar vittles."

Fredo's elbows and knees were grazed, like mine. We hollered all over the Wank Hut and stamped our feet. We had popped the cherries all night long. We were men alright. Except, Fredo's *bragadoccio* throbbed with sincerity.

"We're making plans," he said, of himself and Miss Jane.

"What kind of plans?"

"Summer plans," he said. "Holiday plans."

Fredo's holiday plans were supposed to be the same as mine. What else had we been talking about every day, plodding up and down all those potato fields? Paris; Vienna; Florence. The great cities of Europe by InterRail. Me and Fredo, the Saft Wally English Bastards on Tour.

"I know. But –"

It wasn't Fredo's fault. Cupid had shot his dart. Miss Jane wanted to go somewhere hot, somewhere in the Mediterranean, like Cyprus, just the two of them.

"You traitorous bastard."

"But you said it yourself," said Fredo, "she's a goddess."

As if that was any excuse. The world was full of goddesses. Big Lizzie was a goddess if you saw her in the right light – moonlight, for example, at the end of long, hard roguing season. It was no use. Fredo was smitten. He was in love with Miss Jane.

"Love?" I said. "Big John will set the dogs on you for sure."

Fredo smiled the wide handsome smile that confirmed he'd got away with it again.

"They'll tear you limb from limb," I said, "and then they'll hang up what's left of you to scare the crows."

"Actually," said Fredo, "I've met Big John's dogs and they seem to like me."

* * * * *

We packed our bags, burnt our roguing jeans and locked the Wank Hut for the last time. Down at the farm, as arranged, Davy was in his office, working the columns of his ledger. He poured us two sticky drams and totalled-up what he reckoned we were due. Our six-week season was all there in his ledger – times, dates and locations. Where I had assumed Davy would round the sub-totals down, to the benefit of the Lower Murtry bottom line, he had generously chosen to round them up.

"Fair's fair," he said. "You boys measured up in the squad just fine. You got Big John's Dell through its certificate and that was the icing on the cake for us this year. Thank you."

My season's earnings, after deductions for board and lodging but including bonus, came to £304/17s/6d, rounded up to £305. Fredo's earnings were diminished by the number of evenings he'd skipped off to the squashie with Miss Jane and came to a rounded up £280. Davy snapped the brown paper wrapper off a brick of new fivers and counted out the pristine notes. It was more money than I had ever held in my life. My wallet, a present from Grandad for passing my 'A' levels, was too small for the whole wad. Davy tossed over a couple of elastic bands.

A knock on the door announced Kenny's arrival to take us to Dundee to catch the train south. Davy pulled out another glass and we all four raised a last toast to the best squad in Fife. Davy confirmed that he had known from the start that that Big John's Dell had Desiree rogues in it. The Morrisons had bought it dirt cheap from Old Man Howieson after one of his men tipped a crate of Desiree into the wrong hopper. Entering the Dell for inspection had been nothing but a brazen gamble. I raised my dram high.

"To the season!"

"And to the next one as well," said Fredo. "Bring on those seasons!"

"Lads, lads," sighed Kenny.

At his age, he was disinclined to call down too much *jildi* on the passage of the seasons. Each man had his span of years.

"Aye," said Davy, draining his glass. "Every season has its end, and thank God we've had a good one."

We shook him by the hand again and slung our bags into the back of the Bedford van with mad, faithful Shane. Down the lane and up the brae we went, and over the top for the last time. At the halt sign at Crean big, fat Tam Patterson drove by on his Massey Ferguson with his sheepdog up beside him. Fredo waved and Tam waved back. We knew these folk, and the names of their fields.

At Dundee railway station we bought our tickets and clattered down the same wide stairs that Kenny and his comrades in the Fourth Battalion, the Black Watch, had clattered down some fifty years before. We waited on the same platform where Kenny and Billy Rankin had waited for the train that had taken them to the boat that had taken them to the train that had taken them to the Battle of Loos.

"Thanks Kenny," said Fredo, "thanks for everything."

"Aye," said Kenny. "Take care o' yourself, young Fredo. Stick hard at them 'ologies, you hear. I'll be needing some good doctoring before too long. You too, College. You take good care o' yourself. And mind be in touch about our wee holiday."

I had never been good at goodbyes, always bad at them.

"What wee holiday?" said Fredo.

"I'll tell you later," I said.

"Here's Davy's number," said Kenny, "in case you need to telephone us."

He had written down the Lower Murtry number on the back of the postcard for which he and his squad had posed at Studio Deglasse, Bethune, before the Battle of Loos in 1915. Kenny had given me the last picture of himself in uniform. When I asked if he shouldn't keep it for himself he laughed in my face.

"Why in the holy name o' fuck would a man in my condition want a photograph o' when he was nineteen year old? You keep it, son.

That's what it's for – to remind folk after I'm dead."

I stuffed the postcard in my back pocket as if I didn't give a damn and turned down the platform as if to remove a piece of grit from my eye. When I turned back Kenny had gone.

THE LOST BOYS
OF THE PUNJAB
1915

11 OVER THERE

Lichfield felt like home in all its essentials. There were coats hanging on their hooks and letters in the letter rack, some of them addressed to me. One of them, I knew for sure, contained a bill for breakages from the bursar of St Salvator's Hall of Residence at St. Andrews University. I dropped my roguing bags to the floor.

"Coo-ee! It's me. I'm home."

My mother came bustling out, dusting kitchen work from her hands. She hugged me close then held me at arms' length for a good look-see.

"My, my," she clucked. "You've gone and got all …"

Her eyes shone. She stroked my cheek.

"… Oh, we did miss you, darling!"

The last five months had been our longest separation ever, first the summer term at university, then the roguing.

"You've *grown*," she said.

My mother felt smaller than I remembered, more fragile. There was a ticklish after-effect to her kiss on my cheek. The grey details in her hair had become more pronounced.

"It's good to be back," I gruffed.

The back hall mirror eyed me with suspicion. Big Lizzie was right. Weeks of toasting under the Murtry sun had given me the complexion of a proper Punjabi. I seemed to radiate a sort of blueness. Grandad came out of his study, smelling of whisky, holding his empty water jug.

"Home from the wars is he," he said, "our prodigal?"

Grandad's study had two doors. One of them opened into his surgery, at the front of the house; the other one opened into the small vestibule at the side of the house, which we called the back hall. Since Grandad's retirement, we had started to live more and more 'in the back' while 'the front' turned slowly into a General Practitioner's museum. Grandad took a closer look at me. The emptiness of his water jug warned how far he'd already progressed in his afternoon's course of self-medication.

"Good God," he growled. "You've gone and got all ... You look like a ..."

My mother braced herself. It was her fault I was a chip off the wrong block. She put on her specs in self-defence. During my absence she had taken to wearing them on a ribbon round her neck. Our three generations in the mirror of the back hall reflected precisely why we would never be a typical Lichfield family.

"He looks like a fit, handsome young man," she interjected.

Upstairs, my mother had brightened the desk in my bedroom with garden flowers. I opened the drawers and closed them again. Stacked in an orderly pile was my archive of 'Eagle' comics. Hanging from the ceiling by cotton threads were two Airfix Spitfires pursuing a German Heinkel bomber. I had seemingly outgrown my willingness to suspend my disbelief. If Lichfield was home, how come I felt homesick? The last thing to emerge from my rucksack was the silver pen nib capsule with Kenny's chit inside it, straight from the Battle of Loos.

It was the custom on Fridays in Lichfield for the hippest of the town's teenagers to dawdle home through the centre of town chewing gum before piling into Dobbey's music shop to check out the latest Hit Parade in one of the several sound-proofed listening booths equipped for the purpose. The two Dobbey sons fitted bakelite, ex-Army headphones to the pink ears of the town's hip-most Pop chicks while the old man kept an eye on the fun from behind his repair bench. It was there, in the back of the shop, among the busted Dansette record players and burnt-out Eckovision televisions, that Mr Dobbey hung his stock of second-hand musical instruments. The only thing I knew about guitars was the maximum amount I was prepared to pay for one – fifty bob.

"You might be in luck," he said. "How do you see yourself – Django Reinhardt?"

"Actually," I said, "I was thinking more of Bob Dylan."

"In that case," said Mr Dobbey, "try this Spaniola."

He fished it down with a hook at the end of a pole. I fumbled among its steel strings and brought forth sound. Mr Dobbey returned his attention to his soldering iron. The air around his bench smelled of fireworks.

"What's that you're working on?" I said, strumming with a bit more confidence.

"It's Swedish Uher," said Mr Dobbey. "They make the best tape recorders. Or so they say."

The Uher had a chrome fascia and the superfluity of dials and knobs that placed it at the cutting edge of audio recording technology. Mr Dobbey laced up the tape spools and signalled when he was ready. I dealt the Spaniola a few more strums.

"Ah," he said when nothing happened. "Hold on –"

He fiddled with a switch and the spools began to rotate. The next time I strummed, a red needle quivered in one of the Uher's optics.

Mr Dobbey stopped, rewound and played back the noise I had made. My talent had declared itself.

"I'll take them both," I said.

That evening, while practising the guitar in front of the Uher's microphone, my mother knocked on my bedroom door.

"Have you got a minute, darling? There's something I want to show you."

Hanging inside my mother's wardrobe, curated in lavender silence, were the outfits in which she had been photographed alongside me throughout my boyhood: her fox stole; her tweed suit; the black velvet gown. Two or three times a year my mother would treat herself to something new, making room for it on the rail by discarding whatever had grown tired-looking but always preserving what she regarded as her English classics.

"There are some things here," she said, failing utterly to sound like her normal self, "that your father left you. I think now might be the time, perhaps."

She dragged her dressing table stool across to the wardrobe and clambered aboard to search the top shelf. Next to her bed, on a tea tray set upon a chintz footstool, was the Teasmaid machine that Grandad and I had given her for Christmas two years before.

"I thought it could wait until your twenty-first birthday," she said, returning to earth somewhat awkwardly, "but you're looking so big and grown-up these days."

She handed me a 'Bata' shoe box. It sat in my lap like an unpleasant surprise. As I slipped off the stale rubber band it snapped, stinging my wrist.

"Do you want me to leave?" she asked.

"What? No. Stay. It's fine. I'm fine."

My Punjabi father's watch came out first on a cracked leather strap. Instantly, a hot lump of emotion rose in my throat and lodged there. It was a Corona, 14 jewels, shockproof. My insides fused into a core of numbness.

"It's luminous in the dark," said my mother. "He liked being able to tell the time at night."

My throat burned intensely. These things – my dad's Parker pen, his sandalwood comb – were as close as I was ever going to get to him. I weighed in the palm of my hand a fossilised cricket ball with a split seam. Right at the bottom of the box was a pocket-sized book in a khaki wrapper, the Holy Qu'ran, printed by authority on lightweight paper for the benefit of those employed on government service in the field. Each page of Arabic faced its English translation. The blue-black ink of my father's ownership inscription had faded to the essence of its iron residue. That fading was unbearable.

"It's all him," I croaked.

My mother dabbed her cheeks. I sat on the edge of her bed, concentrating on the dial of the Teasmaid's electric clock. The brand mark was a dancing goblin. The world mocked. My mother's silent tears rolled freely. I scooped my heirlooms back into their box and blundered from the room.

* * * * *

It was a fine, crisp autumn morning the day Billy Rankin fired up his motorbike and rode off to war with Kenny Roberts hanging on the pillion. The Carlton Phoenix was obsolete even in 1914. To start her Billy had to connect the coil, jiggle the carburettor and push her down the Sconsie brae until she burst into life.

"Nobody had a clue about motorbikes in them days," said Kenny, "but I can tell you one thing – yon Phoenix sure made one hell o' a noise. Christ, the racket it made! You could hear it a mile off."

At Wormit Halt, on the Fife side of the Tay Bridge, the lads left the Phoenix under the signal box and waited for the next train to Dundee. The Black Watch was recruiting. The young men of Fife and Angus were flocking to the regiment's drill hall in Bell Street.

"I saw blokes actually fighting to get through the doors," said Kenny. "They were kicking each other to get to the front of the queue. Me and Billy didn't stand a chance. The Black Watch could take its pick, see. The whole o' Scotland knew the Auld Forty Twa, so –"

He bit off the end of his sentence with a fierce glare of disapproval.

"What's that you're up to, College? What's that you're fiddling with?"

We were sitting in the noisy, smoke-filled buffet at London's Victoria Station, waiting for the Dover train to be called. The thing I was fiddling with was the Uher portable tape recorder I had bought with my roguing money to launch my career as the English Bob Dylan.

"Carry on talking," I said. "I'm testing it."

Every time a young woman clicked by on high heels, the red needle quivered in the Uher's sound meter. I liked London's young women with their hairstyles and scarlet lips.

"Testing. Testing. Kenny, you're looking very smart in your jacket and tie."

He lowered his voice and cast a furtive look.

"College, you're not expecting me to speak into that thing are you?"

"Pretend it's not there."

"It is there."

"It's only a microphone."

"It's a fancy fucking contraption and I don't fucking like it. You're embarrassing me."

Swinging London set Kenny on edge. The climate wasn't damp enough to suit his constitution. As for me, I would have been inclined to tarry if we hadn't had such an urgent rendezvous on the other side of the Channel. People who looked like me were clearly able to walk down London's streets without attracting attention or comment.

"Forget it," I said, meaning the tape recorder. "Carry on talking. What were you saying about the Black Watch?"

"Fuck all," said Kenny. "I was saying fuck all about the Black Watch. Fuck off with that fucking thing."

I pressed re-wind.

'College, you're no expecting me to speak into that thing are you?'

"Don't try and tell me that that's me," said Kenny, "because that is *not* what I sound like."

'College, you're no expecting me to speak into that thing are you?'
"Christ, that's awful," said Kenny. "I sound like a fucking choochter."

'I was saying fuck all about the Black Watch.'

"Stop it right now, College."

'I was saying fuck all about the Black Watch.'

"Right now. Or else. And I mean it."

Out on the busy concourse an announcement stirred the gaggle of passengers waiting at platform 12 into a queue. Kenny coughed down the last of his tea and stubbed out his fag.

"Thank fuck for that," he said. "Come on lad, stow it. We're off. *Jildi, jildi.*"

We found a compartment and stowed our kit. I set the Uher on the table between us. It looked very modern and *chic* in its black leather case with thick stitching all the way round. Kenny's suitcase was a battered affair of tartan cardboard. He'd bound it round with an old belt for extra security.

"No turning back now," he said, rubbing his hands. "We're on our way and no mistake, across the narrow seas for king and country."

Whistles blew, the loco hooshed and heaved. Kenny took out his hip flask and set his tin of makings between us. I accepted a pinch of Old Holborn but declined the battle juice. I didn't want to peak too early. As we passed through the suburb of Balham, Kenny's country eye took note of the back gardens, the boughs still full of their summer green.

"Your English season's some way behind ours," he observed. "That's interesting."

With half an eye on the Uher, I contrived to steer his attention back to the war.

"What got me and Billy in the Army in the end," he said, "was friends in high places. The Dalbeattie factor, Frank Leishman, had been in the Boer War with the Black Watch and he was well in with the Bell Street mob. We took his letter with us next time we went and the doc passed us fit in about ten seconds flat. We swore the oath and took the shilling and that was that. *Sodgers!* They sent us straight home. They had no uniforms, see. They had no kit. They gave us a flipping armband. When we got back to Crean, Ma Rankin was at the kitchen window. When she saw our armbands she fainted right down on the spot."

Billy Rankin's mother tried all the arguments she could think of to get him out of the Army. No one would listen. When she went to the lodge at Dalbeattie House, Frank Leishman heard her out with all the attention that a skilled blacksmith's wife deserved but in the end the stark fact remained – Our Billy had signed to be a sodger and no power on God's earth could change that. It didn't matter that he had lied about his age. He was in it. For the duration. Which was no matter, according to the factor, because it was going to be a short, sharp war that would end with the Germans getting the spanking they so richly deserved.

"We had no uniforms," said Kenny, "and we had no kit neither. We took the shilling and they sent us home to get the harvest in. Then, one day, the letter came – report for duty. We had our last night down at The Brig wi' the rest o' the boys and then it was off to the depot for real. Me and Billy thought we'd be going straight across to give the Kaiser what for. They sent us to Forfar, for fucksake. Forfar! For basic training. And it was basic. The instructors were so old they'd forgotten how to drill. They had us out on parade wi' books in their hands – drill books. Talk about the blind leading the blind. The only thing we learned in Forfar was marching. That's the British Army all over. 'No uniforms? Send 'em on a march.' 'No rifles? Send 'em on another march.' "

Outside, the Kentish fields of Siegfried Sassoon's boyhood rolled by, orchards illuminated by bursts of sunshine. The Uher's reels spooled in Kenny's rememberings.

"On our last day, Colonel Walker made a speech to us about how it was a hundred year since the Black Watch had fought at Waterloo. 'The enemy's changed,' he said, 'but it's the same war, men. We are fighting for right against wrong and the position of our nation in the world.' And we all believed him. We cheered like hell. War's a terrible thing, College, but the day I marched through the streets o' Dundee on my way to France wi' the Black Watch behind me – well, that was the proudest day of my young life. *Am Freiceadan Dubh* is the Gaelic for it – Clear the way!"

At Dover, seagulls lined the rails. Rain pattered on the hard shoulders of my new leather jacket, the one I had bought to pose in, moodily, for the photograph that one day soon would adorn the sleeve of my first record album.

"Luxury!" declared Kenny, thumping the vinyl upholstery in a corner of the ferry's passenger lounge. "Last time I crossed over I was in a cattle boat, for fucksake. Pitch black it was, and reeking. Nothing to eat, just the one cup o' tea to last us ten hours. By Christ, we were glad to get to the other side."

I took out one of the books I'd borrowed from Lichfield Public Library about the British military failures of 1915.

"No disrespect," said Kenny, poking his nose in, "but you'll find fuck all in that there book that's worth reading."

I marked my place with a trapped finger.

"I thought you approved of book learning?"

"Don't get me wrong, son. History's all fine and dandy. But see, the thing is College, the war can't be history because I'm still here and I was in it."

The ferry bumped and rolled into the open sea. The cars and lorries strained at their stanchions on the decks below as England's grey cliffs disappeared behind a squall of dirty weather. At Kenny's next offer of a medicinal nip I accepted. I was definitely feeling queasy. Kenny, of course, was immune.

"Here's to *le Continong*," he said, raising a toast. "*La belle France*."

He pressed his nose to a salt-fogged porthole.

"I swore I'd never go back, College, not after what we went through. But here I am and right glad to be on my way. And thank you kindly, son, for coming wi' me."

He gestured towards a break in the murky weather. There may have been something out there, it may have been France, I couldn't tell. Each time I tried to read my war book, the words blurred on the page. I offered Kenny a look at the photos, which he condescended to flick through.

"It's all a wheen of blethers!" he announced. "If it's the war you want, College, just stick wi' me. Did nobody never tell you that war books are all written by officers? You might as well be reading fairy stories."

The ferry came alongside at Calais and docked under the cranes with a fierce reverse churning of its screws. Kenny was one of the first down the gangplank, slithering onto the wet cobbles like an old goat. With a crash of his nailed boot-heels he offered a salute to no one in particular.

"France, by Christ! *Terra firma!* I'm back, boys. 13481 Kenny Roberts reporting for duty."

He shook his head in happy disbelief.

"Pinch me, son," he said, "to show I'm not dreaming. Right-turn. By the left. Quick march. *B'joo, m'soo. B'joo, mam'selle.*"

We brandished our passports and passed through customs. I was proud of my passport and its robust confirmation of my Britannic rights. A French train was waiting, big and square, its compartments full of heavy fittings and framed photographs of the Loire *chateaux*. Kenny seemed to be getting used to the idea that the Uher's rightful traveling space was on the table between us.

"They brought us over in a cattle boat and they had cattle trucks waiting for us when we landed," he said. "No windows, of course. No seats. We were packed in so tight we had to pish where we stood. If you felt a shite coming on, you had to jump off the train and do it behind a tree. Then run like hell to catch up again, with the rest of the mob hanging out the doors taking bets on whether you'd make it or not."

At Lille we transferred to a trim electric commuter train heading for Bethune. I was quietly proud that my approximate French was proving so useful in getting us from A to B. Kenny hopped from one window to the other, searching for something to recognise. Neither of us was sure if we were in France or Belgium. The green shutters on the houses and the slant of their chimneys described an indisputably foreign country.

"Too right they're foreign," said Kenny. "Over here, they eat their horses."

Our train stopped at a small town. The station master stood in his peaked cap by a bank of switches, flicking on the platform lights. Old ladies returning from market headed into the twilight. Kenny turned from his window with wide eyes.

"La Bassee!" he gasped. "Christ, you could have told me. This is Jerry's side of the line."

12 ON THE RAZZLE

The main hotel in Bethune's Grande Place was called La Coupole. Kenny and I were given the twin room under the dome itself. We deposited our passports with the night porter and went straight out on the razzle. The buildings of the Grande Place were *en fete*, swathed in bunting and fairy lights. Fat ladies, toiling under hissing gas lamps, shovelled *frites* and *crepes* into the grasping hands of hungry jostlers. In the centre of the cobbled square, surrounded by tented stalls, soared a black medieval belfry. Kenny elbowed his way through and slapped the base of a weathered buttress. He was back.

"A barber had his shack right here," he said, "right up against this wall. He had a stripey pole and everything. And he must have been the richest barber in the whole o' fucking France because it didn't matter when we showed up, day or night, there was always twenty blokes ahead o' us in the queue."

A close shave was how things always started when Kenny and Our Billy went on the raz before the Battle of Loos. Followed by a good feed of egg and chips, followed by a few bevvies.

"Christ," he said, "but the Froggies watered their beer something chronic. No kidding. You needed an hour's solid drinking hereabouts to get even half-way pished. Then it was off down the Red Lamp to give the whores a look-see. Talk about Sodom and Gomorrah."

We found a table in a busy restaurant and hunkered down. Everyone was eating and smoking and talking at maximum volume. This was Europe, where people stayed up late to enjoy themselves. In that respect, Bethune was the opposite of Lichfield.

"You can leave this bit o' lingo to me," said Kenny, catching the waiter's eye. "*Bon soir, m'soo! Dooze oofs* and your best *pomme frits, si voo play.* And *dooze* of your best *bieres broon* while you're at it, kind sir."

Our brown beers slipped down a treat, followed by two more. Looking round I saw how the place must have been fifty years ago, full of shining faces, Jocks and Muzzie-boys laughing and shouting, sharing their fags and defying their fate. A hundred thousand fighting men came to Bethune for the Battle of Loos, followed by a hundred thousand more.

" 'What passing bells," I said, "'for those who die as cattle?' "

"Thank God for that," said Kenny, pushing aside his empty plate. "I've been ganting for one o' them pomes o' yours ever since we got here."

"Was it like this during the war?" I asked.

I wanted to feel it, or feel something like it.

"Oh aye," said Kenny. "Just like this. But noisier, obviously, on account o' all them English cunts quoting their quotes at us. Christ, you couldn't hear yourself think before the Battle o' Loos thanks to all them pomes flying about."

We left a generous tip and sauntered out into the crowd with full bellies. A well-greased Turk was swallowing flames. A bear danced on a chain. We gawped and cheered and melted into the crowd like the locals when the hat came round. The town's mayor mounted a flagdraped dais and launched into a speech. When the crowd applauded, Kenny and I applauded too. When the mayor's hatted and be-gloved wife switched on the new floodlights we all applauded, long and loud. The old belfry ignited like a rocket, startling the gargoyles and scattering the roosting pigeons. Pretty girls flashed their dark eyes in my direction. I ogled them back and dodged their pesky brothers on their nippy, noisy mopeds.

"Fuck me sideways!" said Kenny, halting in his tracks. "This is where I saw the Prince o' Wales coming out o' yon cake shop."

Bethune's newly refurbished belfry pealed out a carillon. Everyone paused in their *promenade* to look up and listen, except us two.

"He had his bodyguard on one side o' him," said Kenny, "and a red tab on the other, carrying a box o' *gatoo* like so –"

He performed a brief mime of a mincing English staff officer bearing the royal cakes. Then he snapped off a princely salute.

"Lots o' folk called down shite on that boy's head when he abdicated," said Kenny, "not me. I never forgot the salute Prince Edward gave me and Billy right here on this very spot before the Battle o' Loos. He knew what was coming, see. He was on the staff. And here I am, sir. Back again."

Kenny was back, Billy was not. As far as razzling was concerned, I felt myself to be a poor substitute. I knew nothing of machine guns or bombing or whoring. The only person I had ever saluted was an AA patrol man. The barker at the shooting gallery thrust a rifle into Kenny's hands. He surprised us both by failing to win a china doll.

"Fucking air rifles," he said. "Couldn't hit a barn door with one o' them things."

"You're pished you mean."

"Pished? I haven't been pished for years and that's a fact. I'm mellow, College, that's all. I've learned my lesson. Mellow suits me fine these days."

After the municipal fireworks the crowds drifted home down Bethune's side streets like suds down a plug hole. In Rue Voltaire we looked for Studio Deglasse, where Kenny and his squad had posed for their photo fifty years before. There was a jellied pig's head in the window of Baudin's *charcuterie* and a display of autumn novels in Libraire Goffic.

"Gone," said Kenny.

There was a hairdresser's and a hardware store in Rue Voltaire but no photographer's studio. From the direction of the Grande Place came the crash of metal chairs being stacked on metal tables. The *frites* sellers were rolling up their awnings and stowing their cauldrons.

"So," I said, rubbing my hands like a roistering young blade. "Where is this Red Lamp you keep talking about?"

It was too early to go back to the hotel. Kenny led us down a street devoid of fairy-lights. Away from the centre of town, Bethune was a sprawl of proletarian terraces interspersed with schools and the occasional sandy park. We rounded a corner and Kenny stopped to check his bearings against the memories of fifty years ago.

"Aye," he declared, "that's the tobacco factory alright."

He stood in the middle of the street for a better view of a three storied industrial *palazzo*.

"The Froggies took the fag machines out and stacked them in the yard to fit us lot in," he said. "Us and the Fusiliers. Fuck knows how the place was never bombed because Jerry must've known it was a barracks. I can still mind that lovely 'baccy smell inside."

Bethune had survived the war and waxed fat on the surrounding coal fields. Fifty years on, the signs of decline were there to read. A notice on a boarded-up foundry said, '*Pour vendre ou louer.*'

"Aye," conceded Kenny at last. "You're right, lad. I'm lost."

The Red Lamp had gone the same way as Studio Deglasse. The Black Watch and the Royal Scots Fusiliers had hoisted their hipes and marched off forever. We sat on a cold doorstep with the makings of a cigarette between us. I turned up the collar of my leather jacket and listened to the final wail of a departing moped fade into the Woody Guthrie night.

* * * * *

Kenny was first down next morning, tousle-haired and bleary-eyed. He summoned me to his table with an impatient gesture. Out in the *Grande Place*, municipal workmen were dismantling the mayor's rostrum and sweeping up rubbish. The waitress gave me one of those French looks I found so intriguing. There had clearly been a shortage of interesting looking Muzzie-boys in Bethune since 1915. Or was it the effect of my leather jacket and Roy Orbison shades?

"Take them off right now," said Kenny. "They make you look like some kind o' blind cunt."

"You're looking pretty rough yourself this morning," I replied. "Mellow, indeed. You couldn't take your boots off last night."

Kenny had shaved badly and patched his chin with a couple of dabs of lavatory paper. He wanted to march off straight away to the Front, on foot, *toot sweet*. I said we ought to consider getting a map first, and perhaps hire some bikes.

"Bikes?" he sneered. "Fucksake! It hasn't taken you long to go saft after the roguing has it?"

I kept half an eye on the waitress. She wore her glossy hair tied back in a black silk bow. I thought I might be in with a chance, if Kenny would just shut his blethers for a moment and give me an opportunity to exude some charisma. The travelling salesmen finished their breakfasts and went off to their customers. When I caught the waitress' eye she brought *croissants* and a steaming dish of coffee.

"*Merci beaucop, Mam'selle.*"

She was my type exactly. All French women were my type.

"*Je vous en prie, Monsieur. Bon journee.*"

"*A bientot, Mam'selle.*"

"Behave yourself," said Kenny. "You're not here to chase skirt, young College. We're on a job o' work, remember."

The Battle of Loos wasn't History, it was an urgent matter of personal business. Kenny drummed his fingers while I finished eating. He was bursting with suppressed *jildi*. Our Billy and the squad were still out there. My Muzzie-boys were out there too.

* * * * *

We found bikes for hire at Garage Bonneflage but they were large and cumbersome and very out of keeping with my new, cool, troubador's image. After a trial wobble round the block we decided to trade up to a couple of Pintoes, low-octane mopeds engineered in Italy with the limitations of matronly shoppers in mind. The Pinto had a comfortably sprung saddle, capacious panniers and an absolute top speed of 45 kilometres per hour. Padded, peaked crash helmets and leather gauntlets were ten francs extra, per day; the goggles were free. M. Bonneflage's terms, when it came to *les Anglais*, were cash in advance and a deposit of 100 *frongs* each. I stowed the Uher in my pannier, in case some interesting fieldwork should present itself, and followed in Kenny's wake along a straight road leading east.

"I'm pretty sure we came this way," he shouted, above the mopeds' noise, "when we went up to Neuve Chapelle the first time."

We planned to re-fight the year 1915 chronologically, starting with the Battle of Neuve Chapelle before moving on to Loos. But first, Kenny needed to drill into me the rudiments of clutch control and throttling. The only motorbike I had ridden before was Bender's, which I had tried out a few times in and around the Lower Murtry farmyard. Kenny spied a lay-by ahead and we pulled in for a period of instruction.

"Piece o' cake," said Kenny. "It's all about balance. Find your balance on it and you can ride anything."

I accelerated, braked and returned, to get the feel of things. A milk tanker bustled growlingly towards us, followed by a bus. Leaves and scraps of litter fluttered in their double slipstream, the ground shook. This was the actual soil of the continent of Europe we were standing on.

"Kenny," I said, "do you realise we could march to Berlin from here?"

"Hah! I heard that kind o' talk the last time I was here," he replied. "Except yon Jerry had a different idea, didn't he?."

The spirit of the Western Front was upon him. He was 'in it' again, up to his neck in it. This was the road he had marched down fifty years previous, slippery underfoot with the sap and pith of trampled chestnuts. Today, tobacco and maize grew in the fields on either side.

At knee height he spotted a sign in the shape of an arrow.

'Commonwealth War Graves Commission. Billericay Farm
Cemetery. 250 yards.'

"Christ alive!" whooped Kenny. "Billy Rick's farm! Come on, son.
It's all coming back to me."

He hauled his Pinto onto its stand and took off his gauntlets. The
arrow pointed us to a track through the fields.

"Billy Rick's is where I had to come sometimes, College, with
messages from Sergeant Ross. 'Off to Billy Rick's wi' this one, Kenny
my lad, and straight back when it's done.' He was a fine man, Sergeant
Ross, if you stayed on the right side o' him."

I scanned the fields on either side for the bumps and declivities
that might signify old trenches. Kenny gave me a scornful look. There
had been no trenches down this way, not proper ones. Around here,
it had been supply dumps and aid posts. Billericay Farm had been a
Brigade HQ in 1915.

"If there was no message to take back up the line," he said, "you
scrounged off to the cookers to see if there was a brew-up going. They
had it well cushy down here compared to us lot."

The track ended at an iron gate. One angle of the cemetery's
retaining wall incorporated a corner of the original farmhouse.
Weeds sprouted from cracks in the stone sills of four empty windows.
Kenny stood speechless with his *jildi* slowly seeping out of him.

"The last time I was here," he said, "half the roof was still on it." He
took a few dazed, wondering steps.

"The orderly room was down these stairs at the side."

Everything had been smoothed over and made decent. There were no stairs down to the orderly room, only the outline of some brick foundations in a well trimmed lawn.

"Christ!" he said. "They've made it ... beautiful."

The effect of Billericay Farm was supremely picturesque in the morning sunshine. The grass looked greenly unreal. Around the corner massed ranks of white headstones came into view, about oneand-a-half acres of them. We took a row each and began to rogue them, scanning our drills to right and left.

'532441 Private John Herbert James, Royal Scots Fusiliers, 27th September, 1915, Age 20.'

'530580 Private S.D. Nixon, Royal Scots Fusiliers, 27th September, 1915, Age 19.'

The men of Kenny's army stood to attention in due order and discipline. Each man was identified by his regimental badge. Those whose names had died with them lay under the sign of the cross, 'Known Unto God'.

'Lance Corporal Joseph Roberts, R.A.M.C. 11th November, 1915, Age 21.'

I knew what R.A.M.C. stood for – Royal Army Medical Corps, otherwise known as Rob All My Comrades. Sometimes, or so I had read, the wounded would regain consciousness in the care of the R.A.M.C. to find their pockets empty and their watches missing. 'Rob All My Comrades' had struck me as an authentic infantry jest of the time.

"Oh aye?" said Kenny. "Well I can assure you it wasn't 'Rob All My Comrades' when you was lying in the mud with a couple o' Jerry bullets in your arse. Angels o' fucking mercy more like."

Kenny conned the regimental badges with his knowing eye. Each one told a story that ended in death. Under a hawthorn bush against the wall I found a clump of headstones different from the rest. Each of the five slabs was carved with Chinese characters.

"Aye," confirmed Kenny, "we used the Chinks for mending roads. You'd see a whole gang o' them stretched out along the side o' the road, waiting for a gap in the traffic so they could nip out to fill in the pot-holes."

The Chinese graves were nameless, inscrutable.

"It was a world war," explained Kenny. "The whole world was fighting it."

No name, only a number. Each stone bore the same motto.

'A Good Reputation Endures Forever.'

I burned with shame and indignation. These were dogs' graves. If this was how the Chinese had been dealt with, Billericay Farm was probably not the right place to begin my search for Muzzie-boys. The British dead wore their names with pride. Each regiment had its unicorn or lion, its battle cry. The expendable Chinks had merely been disposed of.

"There were a fair few Clearing Stations around here," mused Kenny, "that's why they're all mixed up like this."

Billericay Farm was the place where the stretcher bearers and ambulances had brought those broken in battle. On the graves of those who'd traveled no further, a few mothers and fathers had paid for a modest tribute.

'He lives in our hearts.'

'Till the day breaks.'

Fragrant bushes had been planted at intervals. I crumbled a sprig of Rosemary under my nose. Kenny took a nip from his flask of battle juice.

"Nobody knew what we went through, College. The lads –"

Some sob or blockage stopped his flow, or perhaps it was his dram coming back on him. Kenny passed the flask of battle juice across and I took a sip for solidarity's sake.

"Christ, College, you've no idea what it's like to see your pals hacked down and torn apart and trampled in the fucking mud with their arms and legs blasted off and their eyeballs hanging out and their fucking hair on fire, your own fucking *mates*."

He dropped to one knee, having spotted a weed.

"We died like beasts. Jock or Chinkie made no diff. It was wicked what old Jerry done to us, plain *wicked*."

Looking down on Kenny's sun-mottled scalp reminded me again that I was a young idiot who took life for granted.

'Corporal M. C. Breese, Manchester Regiment, October 17th, 1915, Age 26.'

A pink carnation cast its shadow.

'Sleep, Daddy, until we meet again.'

"And I'm still wondering College," murmured Kenny, "what the explanation for it all might be."

I knew nothing. Billericay Farm had fooled me. Kenny's war could never be explained or tidied up. Kenny had been spared, Corporal Breese taken. That's what battles were for. It wasn't Kenny's fault. But *dulce et decorum est* was no lie, I felt sure of that, Kenny's war did mean something. Fifty years ago it had meant everything to the whole world.

"Aye," he sighed, "but sometimes it seems the same as pointless to me."

He tossed his weed aside. I hadn't found the graves of any Muzzie-boys and Kenny couldn't say where they might be. Ninety-thousand men of the Indian Army had fought on the Western Front. The Hindu dead would have been cremated, I guessed, but not the Muslims. Had they also been given a number and shoveled into some nameless pit? Where were the Muzzie-boys? Kenny held his arms wide and let them flop.

"They're out there somewhere," he said. "We'll find them, College, don't you worry."

The British dead were remembered with whatever scrap of identity could be salvaged. The Chinese had been given their numbers and a respectful motto. The Muslims' recompense in death was nowhere to be seen.

"It would be nice to see some gratitude," I said.

"Gratitude?" said Kenny. "Christ, lad, they were doing their job o' work. They were sodgers. Gratitude doesn't come into it. 'Theirs not to reason why, theirs but to do and die.'"

Kenny had been a soldier, I never would be. But I was entitled to my opinion. The Muzzie-boys were my boys, *dulce et decorum est* for ever. They had to be somewhere. They could not have simply vanished. I would not allow it.

13 PARADISE

Five days after landing in France, the boys of the Fourth Battalion, the Black Watch, were holding trenches. Five days after that Dundee's finest were in their first fight.

"Neuve Chapelle," said Kenny. "That was our baptism o' fire."

Our only guide to the battlefield, cartographically speaking, was a bird's-eye panorama drawn for the 'Daily Mail' in 1915 which was reproduced as an endpaper in one of my library books. Despite Kenny's sneers, it offered a better overview of the Battle of Neuve Chapelle than anything he could come up with. Where French Flanders was concerned, I soon discovered that Kenny's view of the action had been strictly confined to the local and personal.

"Back Street was our first trench," he said. "I can still mind the reek o' it."

As an infantry Private, Kenny had never been shown a map. From the military point of view, his job was to keep his rifle clean and follow the man in front and that's all. Which was why, fifty years later, we had no chance of finding Back Street on the road to Neuve Chapelle. All Kenny could remember was the smell of it. The only man he had to follow was me.

"They set us to work as soon as we got here," he said. "Humping and pumping, digging every night. It near broke my back. And yon Jerry had our range to the inch."

Every night, throughout April and March of 1915, as soon as darkness fell, the roads around Bethune came alive with horses and wagons hauling ammunition and supplies forward for the attack. The British objective was the village of Neuve Chapelle, a township in enemy hands about eight miles due east of Bethune. Against Neuve Chapelle's garrison of barely 1,400 Germans the British Army was massing some 40,000 troops and the biggest concentration of firepower in its history. The aim was to smash the German line and pour cavalry into the gap. Beyond, lay open country and a straight gallop to Berlin.

"Me and Billy thought we'd arrived just in time to win the war," said Kenny. "They set us making ladders, for fucksake."

The war Kenny remembered was not the one I had been reading about, illustrated by arrows on a map. Kenny's war was a strategy-free succession of cold days and freezing nights punctuated by periods of hard labour. Each bend in the road to Neuve Chapelle reminded him of hardships survived through guile and pluck. At each stopping place I scrounged around the fields looking for battlefield scrap – shrapnel balls, shell fragments, any old iron from the trench war that might put me in touch with the real thing, the material legacy, the *actualité*.

"Trenches?" said Kenny. "Christ lad, you couldn't dig trenches round here. Two feet down it's waterlogged. We had to build breastworks. Grouse butts we called them."

Dundee's finest sandbags filled with Flemish mud offered little protection. They were useful for keeping things hid, not for keeping out bullets. The Fourth Black Watch ended up with about four feet of cover, including the mud up to their knees.

"Which was fine for the Gurkhas next door," said Kenny, "because they were fucking midgets. The rest o' us had to crawl."

Nips of battle-juice and regular fag breaks kept us going until, some time after noon, we struck a long straight road. A place called Givenchy lay to the left; a place called Festubert to the right. I stood in dumb homage to the sacred names of the Western Front.

"This is it," confirmed Kenny. "The old front line. This is where your Muzzie-boys were dug in, College, all along this ditch. This side o' the road was ours, over yonder was the Hun."

"This ditch?" I said. "This actual ditch, right here?"

I slid down into it and looked across the road to No Man's Land. This was where, on Wednesday 10th March 1915, the Muzzie-boys, Gurkhas and assorted woggies of the Indian Army had waited out the hours and minutes to Zero, wondering if they were to be their last on earth. Kenny slid down into the ditch beside me.

"See that there? That's Neuve Chapelle. It didn't look like that the last time I saw it."

He scanned the terrain, like the trained observer he was, and pointed to our objective.

"*Estaminet!*" he said. "That's handy. I'm more than ready for some scran."

* * * * *

The café's puddled car park was crowded with tractors and lorries. Inside, we were welcomed with suspicious looks until *le patron* decided we were harmless and gave us a '*Bonjour, messieurs*', at which signal everyone resumed guzzling at full volume. *Le patron's* over-worked wife, or perhaps one of his prematurely aged daughters, found us a space by the window and sat us down in front of a platter of *crudités*.

"And two o' your best *bières broon*, Missus," said Kenny. "*Dooze, si voo play*."

Kenny felt at home immediately, slinging his trench lingo about. I declined a pinch of his Old Holborn tobacco in favour of a Gauloise of my own. With each day in France my tastes were growing more sophisticated.

"See, the theory in the Army," explained Kenny, "was that you needed one o' our lads to every three woggies – to stiffen them up, like. But by Christ, it was the other way round at Neuve Chapelle. It was us new boys that needed the stiffening and your Muzzies that showed us the way."

In the context of the Western Front, 'us' and 'ours', to Kenny Roberts, meant his squad, the Fourth Black Watch, the boys of the Bareilly Brigade or any suchlike constituent unit of the British Expeditionary Force with which he was personally associated. 'Us', to Kenny, meant the lads, men who did it. 'Them' meant everybody else, including the enemy, the Hun, Old Jerry, and anyone on the British side who wasn't pulling his proper weight, including thieving Quartermasters, the red-caps of the Military Police and the politicians and newspaper editors sleeping safely abed in London each night next to their warm, cuddlesome wives. Not to mention every Frog or Belgie making a profit from the harassed British infantryman's all too understandable need for a little rest and recreation from time to time.

"No kidding, College, the Froggies robbed us blind. They charged us rent for our trenches!"

I tasted celeriac for the first time and approved. Everything about the French way of doing things was to my liking. Kenny forked down his egg mayonnaise with hungry relish. I had my own Muzzie-ethnic theories about 'Them' and 'Us' but sensed that now was not the best moment for discussing them.

"At Neuve Chapelle, "said Kenny, "our boys went straight through Old Jerry like a dose o' salts. He never knew what hit him. Seven or eight in the morning it was, bits o' snow on the ground, fuck all breakfast as usual, then suddenly – *wham!* – all hell's let loose. The whole o' Jerry's line goes up in smoke, everything, trees, sandbags, Jerries, the lot. And there's me and our Billy sitting in the best seats in the house, front row. *Wham!* Take that, you fucking Potsdammer! *Wham!* Take that, you sausage-eating cunt. *Wham! Wham! Wham!* We were laughing our silly heads off. We were drunk see, in a manner o' speaking. The ground was shaking from the barrage. Then, as soon as our guns lifted, your Muzzie-boys went over and by Christ I'll never forget the sight. Windy? No chance! Your lads fucking *whored* across. It was murder, actually. The Gurkhas had their knives out. Any Hun bastard that was daft enough to make a stand at Neuve Chapelle was turned to mincemeat on the spot. All it took was half an hour and it was all over – Aha, *mercy b'coo, madame*."

The *plat du jour* laid in front of us was a tender lamb shank in a rich wine gravy. The attacking methods of the Muzzie-boys of fifty years ago immediately went by the board, except for the mopping up. We wiped our plates clean with wads of French bread and sat back with the satisfied air of men who had done themselves proud. Afterwards, returning from the outside lavatory, I walked into an ambush.

"Didier! Chantelle! Regardez – voilà un Indien!"

It was *le patron's* grey-haired scullion. She seized me by the wrist and held on tight, smelling atrociously of the many cats in her life.

"*Ils etaient si beau, si magnifiques, sur votre cheval.* So fine you were, up on your horse."

I saw myself reflected in the black pupils of her adoring eyes.

"*Si courageux,*" she sighed. "*Et vous voilà!*"

Le patron's wife stuck her head round the kitchen door and said something sharp about what needed to be done urgently at the greasy sink. Madame ignored her imperiously and wiped her hands on her apron.

"*Non, non, Madame,*" I pleaded, "*s'il vous plait. Je suis Anglais, pas Indien.* Kenny!"

He sat at our table enjoying the show. The regulars hooted disrespectfully as Madame forced her way to the bar, mounted the brass foot rail and upheld my arm as if I'd won a boxing contest. She had a hairy wart on her chin.

"*Je. Ne. Suis. Pas. Indien,*" I insisted

That made the Frenchmen laugh. The lorry drivers raised ironic glasses. Of course I was an Indian. Everyone in the room could see exactly what I was.

"*Va-z-y, baise-le, Annette! C'est tout a fait ton genre, non?*" Go on, you old bat! Give him a portion. "*Va-z-y, vialle peau!*"

Madame outfaced their derision. They were good-for-nothing eunuchs, *foutues poules mouillees.* Not one of them could stand comparison with any of *les braves soldats Indiens* who had fought to defend *les champs sacres des Flandres* in the days of her youth. I received my due reward in the form of a slobbery kiss on clenched lips and a card slipped into my hand which I stuffed in my pocket without looking. Boozy cheers echoed to the rafters. Kenny's hoots were among the noisiest.

"I'm a wee bit surprised at your taste in women," he said when I regained my seat, all red in the face. "I'd have thought you'd have gone for something a wee bit younger perhaps."

"Thanks for your help," I replied. "Fredo himself couldn't have done less."

Le patron sent over a couple of complimentary cognacs and we raised a toast – *'La belle France'* – to confirm whose side we were on. Madame's valuation of the Muzzie-boys coincided precisely with my own. It was the Sikhs, Gurkhas and Punjabis who had saved the British line in 1915. I was glad there was someone left to re-kindle the flame.

"Oh aye," said Kenny, "it was the Muzzie-boys that took Neuve Chapelle right enough but then what? Eh? Our own top brass went and gave it straight back! We could have been half way to Berlin if the brass hats hadn't ballsed it up. Useless cunts, the whole lot o' them. Fucking useless. They could be guaranteed to make a bollocks of every battle every time."

The short sharp bombardment at Neuve Chapelle caught the Germans by surprise. The speed of the Indians' charge knocked them off balance. But with Jerry on the run, the British hesitated and communications broke down. Clumsiness and indecision allowed the Germans to re-group. The British cavalry did not pour into the gap. The Fourth Black Watch, having been held in reserve throughout, were withdrawn without firing a shot. They were sent to a hamlet called Paradis, to re-fit. Twenty minutes after draining our cognacs we were there, parking our Pintoes in front of a drab Nouveau-Deco monstrosity of a church. Its door was locked and barred. A slate had slid off the roof and smashed on the concrete path.

"So," I said. "So this is Paradise?"

Kenny wasn't listening. A war memorial stood in a chained-off patch of gravel.

'Mort aux Patrie.'

"You wouldn't have thought it possible?" said Kenny, pointing with his unlit cigarette.

Paradis had given twenty-seven of its sons to the Great War, from twenty families. It was hard to imagine how a village consisting of barely fifty dwellings could have raised such a tribute of young men and how it could have survived without them. Their names ran alphabetically from Armand to Thibault. Kenny, having paid his respects, set off down the one and only street and stopped in front of a long brick barn.

'Ferme d'Arnout.'

He looked uncertainly up and down the street. All he had to go on was a hunch he couldn't quite believe in.

"*Paradee*, the Froggies called it. It felt like paradise when we got here, that's for sure – as much grub as you could eat and plenty o' clean straw to kip in. Some o' the lads slept the whole clock round the first day we got here. If it was here."

The farm was arranged Flemish style, around a square yard, with a mouldering midden in the middle. Kenny wanted proof. He had no map, no diary, no evidence in written form. All he had was memories. A net curtain twitched.

"The farm folk know we're here," I said. "Why don't we knock?"

We passed through the arch and an unkempt dog leaped towards us on his rope.

"This is it!" said Kenny.

His bright eye had alighted on a patch of brickwork in the corner of a wall.

"See that? A Jerry shell made a hole right there. We used it as a door."

Monsieur Arnout appeared in person on his doorstep.

"*B'joo, m'soo.*"

The farmer adjusted his belt and asked the nature of our business by sticking out his chin.

"*Mon ami etait ici pendant la guerre,*" I explained. "*C'est un ancien combattant Anglais.*"

"Am I fuck *Anglais,*" interupted Kenny. "*Ecossais, m'soo. E-co-say.*"

Anyone could see what Kenny was, standing to attention with his straight back and slightly bent shoulder. Monsieur Arnout was indifferent, not unfriendly. When Madame Arnout appeared behind him, I explained that Kenny had once lived in their barn, *avec les soldats Ecossais. Le Black Watch. Pendant la guerre. Comprenez-vous?*

Madame, it turned out, had a finer sense of occasion than her husband. Of course we could look around, *bien sur.* She shuffled her feet into a pair of clogs and crossed the yard with us.

"Aye," said Kenny softly, as the barn door creaked open. "This smells like it, right enough."

Time had settled thickly, year by year. Ropes of onions hung from the beams. Otherwise, it was the same as every other barn I had been in that year, full of chaff and straw and old planks waiting to become useful again. Fifty years ago it had been canteen, armoury and dormitory for forty Jocks, one of whom had now come back for a look-see. Kenny wandered over to a cobwebbed corner and hunkered down. Madame Arnout left us to it.

"You're standing right where Ian King copped his," said Kenny nodding towards to the postern in the barn door behind me. "Wee Sammy Chisholm was cleaning his hype and all of a sudden – *bang*! – there's Kingy's thumb gone. That was the luckiest blighty one I ever saw. They had to hold a Court Martial to prove it wasn't self inflicted."

Outside, where Kingy's thumb had never been found, hens clucked and strutted round the dung heap. Inside, squatting between stacked baskets of apples and a family of rusty bikes, Kenny remembered the place where he and our Billy had supped and kipped, played cards, shared parcels and squabbled over rations and rum. I mooched around, picking up tools and putting them down again. I unfolded a canvas nosebag and it disintegrated in my hands like a mummified concertina. Some of the original bricks still bore their wartime graffiti. I lit a match and the outline of a maple leaf flared into focus.

'Sweet Jesus, hear my prayer. D. B. C. Montreal. 12. XI. 15.'

"Aye, we shared Paradise with all sorts," said Kenny. "Canucks, mainly. They all got paid more than we did. Except your Muzzieboys, o' course."

A pre-twilight chill crept in from the fields. Madame re-appeared in the yard and we emerged blinking, brushing dead insects from our hair.

"*Tray bon, Madame,*" said Kenny. "Very much appreciated. *Remercy b'coo.* We're very grateful, me and the lads. God bless you, Missus."

Every day during the Great War, in wrecked barns all over France and Flanders, men of all colours and creeds had prayed to their gods and crawled out after the bombardment to count the cost. Recklessly, Kenny grabbed Madame Arnout and kissed her appled cheeks. She reddened as much as he did. Then she took both his hands in hers.

"Ce n'est rien, Monsieur. C'est nous qui vous remercions. Vous avez sauve la ferme, les Ecossais, les Indiens. Merci beaucoup."

That was the Great War in a nutshell. In 1914, millions of men who had no quarrel with the Kaiser felt it their duty to win back the fields, barns and factories he had seized in France and Belgium and was refusing to give back. They stayed until that job of work was done and then they departed, with thanks.

14 THEM AND US

As well as illuminating their restored belfry with floodlights, the burgesses of Bethune had invested in a complete interior refurbishment. The ground floor chamber once used for taxing the region's cheese-mongers had been turned into a picture gallery for the benefit of local artists. In the corner was a spiral of stone steps permitting access to the upper storeys. From the top battlement we surveyed the cobbled acre of the Grande Place below, enclosed by narrow, authentic-looking medieval facades, all dating from the 1920s. Kenny gazed over the chimney tops.

"It's like –"

The morning mist had rolled away, revealing French Flanders like an open book. Out there, under the tobacco fields and damp orchards, was The Line, the ghostly remnant of a landscape that had stained Kenny's dreams for years. He frowned dizzily.

"Being up here," he said, "is like being an angel. In a manner o' speaking."

All Kenny had seen of the war was the trench he'd been in or the back of the man in front of him. It beggared his powers of comprehension to stand with the whole battlefield displayed like a play rug. Beyond the edge of town, roads and railways receded into the distance. Villages huddled round their ugly, rebuilt churches.

"It was nothing like this in my young day."

The trenches, traverses, dugouts and saps had been ploughed in and harrowed flat.

"You never saw a stitch o' greenery when we was here. Everything was mud. Everything was grey."

" 'Cities and thrones and powers …' " I intoned.

"What?"

It was another of my dredged-up poetic inspirations. Kenny was seeing his war as no Scottish foot-slogger had ever seen it before. A small plaque had been set into the battlement.

Pendant la Premiere Guerre Mondiale, ce belfroi etait un poste d'observation d'ou les troupes Britanniques surveillerant les lignes Allemandes entré 1915 et 1918.

"Aye," said Kenny. "It was the artillery that won that war for us. 'Artillery conquers, infantry occupies'. Did you ever come across that in one o' your war books?"

The British artillery had fought a long, hard war. The infantry fought a harder one.

"Once we'd seen how it was at Neuve Chapelle," said Kenny, "me and Billy started looking for a way out. It was as plain as the nose on your face – the infantry had no fucking chance. The infantry had to sit there and take it. That wasn't the job for us two. I mean, standing in mud with only barbed wire for protection, what odds on that, eh?"

Billy Rankin, the motorcycle pioneer, tried to wangle himself a job as a despatch rider. Kenny, knowing a fair bit about horse-work, applied for a transfer to the Transport. Their chance, when it came, was with the bombers.

"See, they'd set up this training school at a place called Whiskers. It felt like going on holiday until we got there. On our first morning, Sergeant Sullivan had us out on parade before breakfast. 'You are here, gentlemen, to learn how to kill Huns. And that process begins, as we all know, with a five mile march. So get fell in.' He had a cold eye for his fellow man did Sergeant Sullivan. We thanked him for that in the end."

After the failure at Neuve Chapelle, the British Army set about learning its lessons. The Germans, once they had got over their initial surprise, had contained the British advance by their superiority in weapons and tactics. They had trench mortars, the British had none. The Germans had hand grenades, the British had none. The Germans had gas, the British had none, although they were working on it.

"Old Jerry was miles ahead o' us," said Kenny. "He had rifle grenades, for fucksake. He could hit us from two hundred yards away. At the start o' 1915 we were making bombs from old jam tins. No wonder they had to send us to trench school. Our boys knew fuck all."

There was a click and a whirr in the bell loft above us. Doves scattered as one clangorous *DONGGGG!!!* followed another. The toysized people in the Grande Place checked their watches and looked up.

"It's a flipping miracle," shouted Kenny. "Bethune's a phoenix from the flames and no mistake."

"Ashes," I shouted back. "Strictly speaking, Kenny, the phoenix rises from the ashes."

The word 'phoenix' brought our Billy to mind, and his motorbike. Where was he? Missing in action. What had happened? Kenny could not say, or wouldn't.

"No disrespect, young College, but I wish he was here with me right now to see all this."

Kenny stood above the battle with his story locked inside and a promise to keep. Somewhere out there was the last place on earth trodden by his best friend Billy Rankin. He screwed a knuckle into his raptor's eye.

"It's my ducts," he explained, working a tear sideways. "All my ducts are blocked. I'm fucked, College. I'm done in. After you on the way down, son, I'll need you to lean on."

* * * * *

The first lesson Kenny and Billy learnt at Wisques was not to be late for class if you didn't want Sergeant Sullivan putting you on bread and water for three days. The second lesson they learned was that, as far as the trench war was concerned, the rifle and bayonet had had their day. It was the bomb and the machine gun that would win the next battle.

"The first bomb they gave us was Japanese," said Kenny. "They were intending to copy it, for ourselves like, but they soon changed their minds when they saw how dangerous it was. The fuse on that Jap contraption was fucking lethal. Unless it was fitted just right the slightest knock would set it off. That Jap Mark One was a total fucking menace. No wonder they got rid of it."

Kenny no longer reacted to the sight of the Uher like a frightened cat. Fragments of squad lore re-surfaced as the *bières brunes* flowed. As well as bombs, Kenny and Billy had been taught the rudiments of the trench mortar and the machine gun.

"You had these two wooden handles on the Vickers, and you fired it with your thumbs. That was the first thing you learned about the

Vickers – no trigger. Second thing was, she was very temperamental. 'Moody as a French whore,' said Sergeant Sullivan, 'but with more moving parts.' It took a fair bit o' shooting to get to know your Vickers. Sergeant Sullivan timed everything we did on his stopwatch."

It didn't matter whether you were training with the bomb or the machine gun, there was no arguing with Sergeant Sullivan. If you were slow, you did it again. He never relaxed. Each squad had to function in battle with the quick-fire precision of the weapons it served.

"They built this long hut with no windows in it and doors at both ends. Then they filled it with all kinds o' rubbish and turned on the gas. You had one minute, sixty seconds, to get in one end and out the other. Well, there was this one chap, a big lad called Lennon from down south, who just couldn't face the gas. He was a good lad at the bombing and the Vickers but they told him he would fail the course for sure if he didn't pass the gas test. He says, 'Well you might as well a-fail me right now, Sarjint, coz I ain't a-goin' in there, I'd rather die.' And Sergeant Sullivan says to him, 'Right, lad. Follow me.' And he took some bloke's gas hood off him and put it on himself. Then he took Lennon by the hand and led him into that gas hut like a lamb. And when they got out the other side Sergeant Sullivan took off his hood and he says, 'That's a set of brass buttons you owe me, Lennon.' And so it was, because the gas was peeling the shine off his buttons right in front of our eyes. Rotten pears is what that gas smelled of. I can smell it now."

Kenny looked into his *bière brune* and coughed. The deep gall remained inside.

"That gas, College – it'll put me in my grave, I swear."

* * * * *

After the Battle of Neuve Chapelle, the Fourth Black Watch was rested but the Punjabis, Sikhs and Gurkhas were kept in the line. There were not enough men on the British side to give everyone the respite they needed. Every attack was followed by a counter-attack. It was called attrition, the war of *materiel*. The odds were in Jerry's favour. He had more guns, more ammunition, more men. Wherever there was a slight advantage of terrain, he held that too.

"Why do you think it was called the Western Front?" said Kenny. "It wasn't west to us lot, was it? It wasn't west to the Froggies neither. It was the Ger-boys who decided which front it was, the bastards. The whole Western Front was theirs."

The Indian Army began arriving in France towards the end of 1914. By November, there were 35,000 of them in the line. By Christmas, they'd lost 5,000 casualties. By the time they'd got through Neuve Chapelle, in March 1915, the casualty figure was 14,000. By the end of June, 1915, the number was 29,000. Casualties at such a rate – an average of 100 per day killed, wounded or missing – were unsustainable. The Indians had been trained for a hot, dusty war of skirmish and movement. They were not organised to deal with a muddy war of attrition five thousand miles from home. There was only one sure source of reinforcement for the Indi-boys when they needed beefing up for the Battle of Loos – British Territorials.

"Honorary woggies?" said Kenny, checking that he'd heard me correctly. "You're saying we were *honorary woggies*?"

The chronic shortage of men for the trenches had thrown the British Army's traditional notions of Them and Us into reverse. To keep the Muzzies up to strength they were given Jock reinforcements.

"Them and us?" said Kenny. "What the fuck are you talking about?"

Kenny had never looked at his war from the point of view of gross manpower but that was precisely the problem facing the British Army in 1915. The Germans were killing the British faster than they could be replaced by Lord Kitchener's as-yet untrained volunteers. The Indians had been rushed into the line to buy time but in the absence of reinforcements they too were being bled dry. The only men available were the lads of the Territorial Force, trained primarily for home defence. The Black Watch, the Connaught Rangers and the Leicestershires were among the first to be drafted in. They had more in common with the Huns than their Muzzie-boy comrades.

"Don't you see what I'm getting at?"

"No," said Kenny. "Is this another one o' your silly jisms you're leading up to?"

"Kenny, what was the name of the infantry brigade they put you in, the Fourth Black Watch?"

"The Bareilly Brigade. That was our mob."

"Were the other battalions in the Bareilly Brigade from Scotland?"

"They were not."

"Where is Bareilly?"

"Fuck knows."

"It's in India."

Bareilly was one of the oldest garrisons of the British Raj. It was manned by Gurkhas and Dogras as well as the Punjabis and Pathans of the 58th Vaughan's Rifles.

"The survival of the Empire was at stake, Kenny. Some wore the kilt, some wore the turban. As long as a man could hoist a hype in 1915 no one cared. By the time you boys had got Neuve Chapelle out of the way and were ready to fight the Battle of Loos, half the men in the Indian brigades were white boys like you."

"Honorary *woggies*?" said Kenny.

Some people were born that way, others had it thrust upon them.

"You and the Muzzie-boys, you wore the same uniform, correct?"

"Aye, lad. We did. *'Theirs not to reason why, theirs but to do or die.'* You're damned right, young College. All blood runs red."

His chair suddenly shot back into the chair behind him. Kenny stood with his glass upraised.

" 'A man's a man for a' that.' " he proclaimed.

Everyone in the bar turned to look. Kenny stared back with fierce loyalty. I almost wished I'd kept my mouth shut.

"The woggies forever, ladies and gentlemen. And I'm damned proud to be one. *Je m'apelle Muzzie-boy, m'soo.* Here's to the Muzzieboys and God bless 'em all."

It was the eve of battle, September 24th, 1965. I raised my own glass, Kirkbuddo-style.

"Scotland the Brave!" I answered. "Scotland the Brave for ever!"

15 SCOTLAND THE BRAVE

Next morning in Bethune, a new waitress was on duty in La Coupole's dining room, demure, dark haired, adroit at avoiding eye contact. Then Kenny arrived. He had fixed the red hackle of the Black Watch to his roguer's flat cap with a safety pin.

"You're looking the part," I said.

Kenny's medals, Pip, Squeak and Wilfred, clinked on his chest.

"Flipping piece o' puff pastry," he said, tearing into a croissant he had no intention of eating. "What kind o' breakfast is a *kwasong* for a fighting man, for fucksake?"

Saturday, 25th of September, 1915, had been the biggest day in Kenny's life. Fifty years on, to the day, it was still out there, waiting for him.

"Biggest battle in Scottish history," he declared. "And I was in it, right in it."

Unfortunately for Scottish history, the Battle of Loos had been conceived at a time when the British Army was the junior partner in a coalition dominated by the French, and what the French wanted at Loos was a diversion to distract the Germans from their own big push further south.

"They didn't tell us that though, did they?" said Kenny. "They didn't tell us the whole show was a distraction. Thank you, Papa Joffre. Ta very much. Bet you've never read that in any war book."

I had, of course, read exactly that. The painful gestation and botched delivery of the Battle of Loos had been neither ignored nor glossed over in any of my war books. Kenny switched his attention to a crusty baguette.

"They gave us iron rations before the off," he said, "and extra sandbags. And every third man was given a pick or shovel to carry as well as his hype. Except for us bombers o' course. We were held back for when we was needed."

The Muzzie-boys and Jocks of the Bareilly Brigade left their billets around Bethune on Friday, 24th September, 1915, and marched to their trenches down muddy country roads jammed solid with troops and transport. To the old hands it felt exactly like a re-run of Neuve Chapelle. At a place on the map called Epinette Farm, the Bareillys stopped for a last legal cigarette then burrowed into a long communication trench called Winchester Street that led to the front line near a village called Mauquissait.

"And here's another thing," said Kenny, licking a blob of strawberry jam off the point of his knife, "the top general in charge at Loos was a Fifer called Dougie Haig. Same as Haig's whisky, down at Markinch. That's his folk. And a very acceptable brew it is in my opinion."

General Sir Douglas Haig disliked the idea of fighting a battle in the coal mines around Loos. For a start, the whole area was pancake flat and devoid of cover apart from slag heaps, nearly all of which had been occupied and fortified by the Germans. Haig did not have enough heavy guns or high explosive ammunition to prepare the ground. *Tant pis.* Too bad. The French *generalissimo*, Papa Joffre, had laid his plans. Reasons of grand strategy demanded a big effort from the Allies as 1915 drew to a close. On the Eastern Front, the Germans had stopped the much-vaunted Russian steamroller in its tracks.

In the south, the combined French and British assault against the Turks at Gallipoli had developed into a stalemate. The Western Front remained the one place where the Allies might yet be able to land a blow. Grand strategy demanded that the British fit in with French plans and do their best.

"Strategy?" said Kenny. "That's an officer's word. It's the ranks who do the dirty work."

The dirty work facing Haig's army at Loos was to get across No Man's Land in the face of concentrated German firepower. That's where the gas came in. The British didn't have a lot but they might have enough. The prevailing wind in Flanders was westerly, more often with the British than against them. Perhaps Haig could compensate for his deficiencies in artillery by sending his infantry across behind a cloud of gas? After the usual feint, of course. That was the doctrine in 1915 – feint attacks to distract the enemy and draw off his reserves before the main thrust went in. Joffre had delegated his feint to the British; the British delegated theirs to Kenny and our Billy, amongst others.

"Expendable," said Kenny, "that's what we were."

"In the first two hours of the Battle of Loos," I said, "the British suffered more casualties than the total on both sides on D-Day, 1944." It was an interesting fact I had come across in one of my war books.

Kenny looked at me.

"And which one o' them fights was you at, young College?"

"Fine," I said. "Have it your way. Sorry I spoke."

Clearly, the fiftieth anniversary of the Battle of Loos was the wrong day for a saft, wally English bastard like me to have anything interesting to say about the biggest battle in Scottish history. I took out the map I had bought.

"Map?" said Kenny. "Christ lad, we don't need no map. I was there, remember."

He poured a slug of battle juice into the last of his breakfast coffee and swigged it down.

"I'll meet you out the back in five minutes," he said, "after attending to a call o' Nature."

The waitress watched him leave, medals clinking. I felt proud of him, and protective. Seeing Kenny from behind reminded me how old he was. He had one year left of his Biblical span. The waitress allowed me to catch her eye.

"*Votre ami*?" she said.

"Old soldier," I said, "*Vieux soldat*. We're going to the battlefields. *Champs des battailes*."

"*Ah oui*," she said. "*Vous êtes touristes Anglais?*"

The waitress was not what Fredo would have called a looker but I was instantly keen. Clearly, after Big Lizzie, my life was never going to be the same again.

"*Mon ami est un Ecossais*," I said. "Scotland the Brave, *Mam'selle*."

"*Ah oui*," she said. "*Et vous, Monsieur. Vous est Indien?*"

"*Mais oui. Bien sur. Je suis un Indien*."

If she was interested in a *pukka* woggie, why not?

"*Ah. Tres bon. Au revoir, Monsieur l'Indien. Bon journée*."

Of course she was interested. I had a leather jacket and Roy Orbison shades. I was exotic and interesting and fluent in Franglais.

"Oh aye," agreed Kenny, "a wee bit o' lingo goes down well wi' the *mam'selles* around here. I learned that some time ago."

My waitress had a grandma somewhere who would remember the Jocks in their kilts. Kenny might even have met her, one fine night in Bethune while out on the razzle.

"Will you please get a shift on," he snarled, "and stop your blethers. I'm not interested in no young chit's French granny. I can make my own arrangements in that department, thank you very much."

I checked the map. The hamlet marked as Mauquissait was no more than a twenty minute ride away by Pinto. Just seeing the name gave me a queer feeling. I felt the need to salute. I saluted Kenny.

"Aye," he said, saluting me back, "there's a job o' work to be done today and we're the boys to do it."

I raised my leather gauntlet in the direction of the front line.

" 'There is not anything more wonderful,'" I intoned, " 'than the sight of a great people moving towards the deep of an unguessed and unfeared future ...' "

"Aye, that's a good one," said Kenny. "You keep quoting your quotes, young College, and we'll get through today just fine. Now, let's be putting some *jildi* into it, for fucksake."

* * * * *

Mauquissait turned out to be more of a sparsely populated curve in the road than an actual hamlet. It consisted of a row of brick cottages, a large chicken run and a collection of out-houses in varying degrees of collapse. A couple of sprawling farms on either side of the road completed the picture. The obligatory muddy hound came out to investigate our arrival but quickly got bored after sniffing the Pintoes' tyres. We made a fuss of him, for Shane's sake, and wondered how that noble beast might be faring back home. That good woman, Wilma, had agreed to look after him. I smoked a Gauloise while Kenny walked up and down in an attempt to fix his bearings.

"It's the objective we need," he muttered. "Where's that fucking *moolan*?"

The Moulin de Pietre had been Jerry's strongest redoubt in the Mauquissait sector. It was a ruined mill, strongly wired and entrenched, behind the German front line. Fifty years on, all Kenny felt able to say was that he thought Jerry's actual front line might have been somewhere in front of the brick cottages.

"Are you sure?"

"Mebbe."

"In this field of cauliflowers?"

"Mill Trench we called it."

There was no trench, no parapet, no wire. Nowhere could we see any sign of the Bareilly Brigade. The attacking infantry at Mauquissait had comprised three battalions – Leicesters, Gurkhas and the Black Watch. The Punjabi Muslims of the 58th Vaughan's Rifles had been held back as reserve.

"The Leicesters were on our right," said Kenny, "The Gurkhas on our left. Christ, them Leicesters were a rough lot. Some o' them went over the top carrying meat cleavers, no kidding."

At 0540 hours, Saturday, 25th September, 1915, the taps were turned on and chlorine gas hissed out from canisters hidden in the British front line. The gas formed a greenish-yellowish cloud that billowed up and toppled over into No Man's Land. Some of it began to drift towards the German line, some of it stayed where it was. The German machine gunners opened up to check their range. The British infantry – those who hadn't breathed in their own gas – checked their gas hoods.

"Billy checked mine," said Kenny, "and I checked his. You left it until the last minute because as soon as that gas hood was on you started sweating like a pig and when those two wee portholes steamed up inside you couldn't see a thing."

At 0548 hours the final British bombardment opened with a heartening crash. Weeks of carefully hoarded ammunition went skyward in a roar of smoke and flame.

"We felt it through our boots," said Kenny. "The whole trench started to shake."

At 0600 hours the whistles blew and the two leading Companies of the Black Watch swarmed up their ladders. Smoke candles had been lit. The brigade engineers were firing phosphorous bombs from mechanical catapults. Two field guns had been wrestled into the front line and they too were banging away, adding to the smoke screen.

"Talk about the blind leading the blind," said Kenny, "you couldn't see a thing. Us bombers just sat there. Sergeant Ross was lying out on the parapet, waiting for the order."

A tractor came round the bend and Kenny jumped the ditch to flag it down.

"B'joo M'soo, Moolan de Pietre?" he inquired. "Oo là là?"

The tractor-man appraised Kenny from under the bent peak of his Flemish farmer's cap. Kenny's red hackle and the medals on his chest said everything about the purpose of our visit. The tractor man pointed east.

"*C'est l'endroit que vous cherchez. La ou il y avait le Moulin.*"

A mill had certainly existed over there, once upon a time, at the far end of the two long fields behind the orchard. But it had gone, *kaput, fini,* many years ago, *pendant la guerre.*

"*Oui, oui,*" said Kenny enthusiastically. "*Pendant la guerre. Moolan de Pietre.*"

Nearly half-mile away, down where the mist thickened almost to opacity, stood a row of tall poplars. Behind them was the vague shape of a building. Someone had built a farm on the site of the old mill.

"*Un lieu maudit, a mon avis,*" said the tractor man. "*Il n'a pas porte chance a Malbrancque.*"

"So," said Kenny, adjusting his mental calculations, "if that there is the site o' the objective, then that there –"

He pointed to a scrap of hedge alongside the cauliflowers –

"That there is Mill Trench!"

Kenny gave the tractor man the thumbs up.

"*Mercy, M'soo,*" he said. "*Tray bon.* You're a top man, sir. *Tray bon. Tray bon.*"

We shook hands all round and the tractor man kicked in the tractor's clutch pedal. He was taking a consignment of empty boxes to a squad of cabbage pickers. We could just make out their swaddled forms through the mist.

"*Oo là là,*" I said. "Your *parly-voo* is coming on a treat, *m'soo.*"

"I'd be watching that sharp tongue o' yours, College, if you don't want a kick up *la derrière.*"

As we jumped the ditch, the leather-trussed Uher bounced behind me like a spare buttock. Scattered in the drills between the fog-soaked cauliflowers were reminders of the bombardment of fifty years ago, shrapnel balls and fragments of old shell cases. I held up a strand of barbed wire, brittle with rust. It snapped like a twist of barley sugar. Kenny kept one eye on the Moulin, to keep us straight. I could see the Gurkhas and Leicesters quite clearly. The Gurkhas wore slouch hats and wielded *kukris*, the Leicesters carried meat cleavers. I was a nineteen-year old subaltern, with a silver whistle to my lips –

"No, lad," said Kenny. "There was no whistle for us that day."

There was no whistle for the bombers. Their job was to wait until the first, second and third waves of infantry had gone over, then to follow up and clear out any Germans remaining.

"It sounded great in training," said Kenny. "Winkle out the survivors, then bomb your way up the flanks. They'd given us a new bomb for the job, the Number Fifteen. We called them cricket balls because that was about the size o' them. Fucking useless they were."

No one in England knew how to make hand grenades in 1915. The cricket ball was a hasty, unreliable improvisation designed to be churned out cheaply in numbers.

"We trained with them for a week before the battle and at least a quarter o' them turned out to be duds. If the slightest bit o' damp got into the cricket ball, it was useless."

We advanced up our drills like roguers, scanning right and left.

"As soon as the gas shifted," said Kenny, "the first thing we looked for was gaps in Jerry's wire. Our guns had shot his breastworks to fuck. By the time we got to his old front line, our machine guns were in action and everything looked ticketty-boo."

Details of the re-built Moulin slowly became visible. There was a barn next to the big house, and some sort of tall chimney.

"What do you think?" said Kenny, casting around for Jerry's front line. "Could this be it?"

Old Jerry was nowhere to be seen. Kenny looked back the way we'd come. The tide of Peace had swept away his battlefield. I pointed to a couple of concrete bunkers over by the cabbages.

"Do you remember them?"

"Of course I fucking remember them," snapped Kenny. "One o' them was Salt Post, the other one was Pepper."

But was it here or somewhere else that Kenny had known Salt and Pepper Post? Fifty years of telling the tale had blurred the lie of the land.

"To be honest, College," he said, "I am a wee bit puzzled. See, being in trenches all day we never saw a thing. The only time we got out on top was at night and what could we see in the dark? Fuck all, right? That's why, now that I'm stood here again –"

Kenny gazed towards the Moulin. That was real enough. There could be no doubts about the Moulin. It looked gaunt and forbidding.

"I can tell you one thing for sure," he said. "When we got to Jerry's front line I jumped in and landed on a dead one. Christ, the look on his face! His helmet was smashed right down between his eyes. No blood mind, just his brains dripping down like rice pud."

Sideways through the mist, the cabbage squad had come to a halt. They had finished stacking the empty crates and were now sharing a fag break in the lee of the empty trailer.

"I feel like a ghost," said Kenny, looking round with wide, uncertain eyes.

I could see that, as far as the Bareilly Brigade's fiftieth anniversary reunion was concerned, the two of us hardly constituted a jamboree. On the other hand, where else would Kenny rather be on this very day?

"All the same," he said, "it feels kind of –"

The flat polders felt damp and spooky. The mist was getting thicker. Was that why Kenny had brought me along, for human warmth? We set off again, following the ghost track of the Bareilly Brigade's bayonet charge.

"That was our first big mistake," said Kenny. "Our lads went for the second line too early."

With the leading wave of gas-hooded infantry meeting only slight resistance, the Black Watch, Leicesters and Gurkhas had barely paused at the German front line before pressing on towards the Moulin. They should have waited for the bombers to consolidate.

"The thing was," said Kenny, "Captain Moodie had a bet on with Captain Coupar as to which one o' them would get to the Moulin first so 'fuck consolidation' was their watchword. Fair enough. Plus, they had to keep up with our barrage. But as soon as they set off, up popped old Jerry's snipers. That's when the officers started dropping. They wore the hackle, see. It made them targets."

The crop planted between the German first and second lines was new to me. It looked like some kind of mutant turnip.

"Sugar beet," said Kenny. "Davy's thinking of mebbe trying it himself next year. There's talk o' building a sugar factory in Cupar."

Memories of Fife came crowding in. These fields once marked the absolute edge of the universe for a generation of Scottish farmboys.

The Moulin de Pietre was as close to us now as two long throws of a cricket ball. I realised the truth of a phrase I'd come across in one of my war books and discounted without thinking: war is a bloody game.

"It must've been about here," said Kenny, halting in his drill, "that Jerry really got his guns onto us. High explosive mixed wi' shrapnel. Big bastards. As soon as our third wave went across, old Jerry boxed us in. No one could get across after that. No runners. No stretcher bearers. The wounded were lying all over the place. Arms off. Legs off. Bits hanging out. Heads off. Fucksake. You just had to kick on through. You couldn't stop for the wounded. It was against our training. If the wounded got in your way you had to tread on them."

The Black Watch had been drilled to keep up with the artillery barrage, which was lifting forward every four minutes. That was the timetable by which the artillery would 'walk' the Bareilly Brigade through Jerry's lines and into the Moulin, two-hundred-and-fifty yards every four minutes.

"And we'd have made it, by Christ, if all o' Jerry's wire had been cut."

Kenny stared at the Moulin with his fists clenched. Once the bombers had cleared out the German first line trench – by throwing grenades into any cranny or hole where a Jerry might be lurking – they waited with the machine guns to be ordered forward. No orders came. Instead of moving into the attack, the bombers stayed put and watched.

"There was too much wire. Jerry had two belts o' it. Thick stuff. Loads of it."

Kenny marked a line on his chest to show the height of the German barbed wire in front of the Moulin. The British guns had hardly tickled it.

"The lads in front were shouting, 'Back boys, back! The wire's no cut!' but the rest o' them kept on piling in. They had no choice, nowhere to go. There was no cover anywhere."

With the gas blown away and their gas-hoods off, Captains Coupar and Moodie raced for the Moulin. The Black Watch was raring for a fight. Kenny bit his lip.

"When the second and third waves reached that wire –"

He looked back the way we had come. It was the wind again, messing with his blocked ducts.

"There was only one plan, see. Gas, barrage, advance. That was what we had trained for. So when our lads found the wire in front o' them untouched –"

Kenny glared down at the sugar beet.

"Ach, you couldn't bear to watch. They were running up and down that wire like trapped rabbits. It was a massacre, College. We lost all the officers and half the men."

As Captain Coupar and Captain Moodie and their men reached the wire in front of the Moulin, the British barrage lifted forward on schedule. The Germans came up from their fortified cellars with machine guns. Jocks and Gurkhas tore at the wire with their bare hands. They dug into the earth with their fingers. They dug with their bayonets. There was no escape. Jerry's machine guns opened up at point blank range.

"Jesus God, you couldn't bear to watch. It was pure slaughter.

Napoo for ever, the Fourth Battalion. Some o' the boys took so many rounds they just fell apart, all shot to rags."

It was the wire that beat them, and Jerry's machine guns. It was the gas. It was the shrapnel.

"From that minute on, College, it was every man for himself."

We approached the Moulin in choked silence. Conflicting emotions boiled within me, compassion, horror and righteous indignation. The tall chimney of the Moulin's big house rose almost as high as the poplars. The field of sugar beet ended with an abrupt drop into a steep-sided drainage channel.

"Fucksake!" said Kenny. "The Layes brook!"

We had reached the heart of battle, the zone of certain death.

"The dead and wounded were everywhere," said Kenny, wretchedly. "In the mud. On the wire. Kilts agley. White arses everywhere you looked. Jerry gave us no quarter that day."

The Layes brook gurgled clear and calm in its sandy bed. The stream in front of the Moulin farm was as wide as a moat. Rat holes showed between tangled tree roots. We saw it through the eyes of the Moulin's defenders, from Jerry's point of view. He had dominated the battlefield. Here, he had tuned a French miller's home into an abattoir.

16 FIGHTING RETREAT

Ivy ran riot across the walls and roofs of the farm the Malbrancque family had re-built after the Great War on the site of their razed *moulin*. Bales of straw lay rotting in the yard. In one corner, the wooden walls of a big, square threshing machine had cracked asunder and collapsed onto steel-rimmed wheels. No one remained to separate the wheat from the chaff.

"Aye, the farm must've turned against him," said Kenny, kicking the tines of a twisted harrow. "Or mebbe he took to drink. It happens, first one thing, then another, then bankrupt."

By the step of the farmhouse back door was a pet's bowl filled with dried leaves. Inside the wrecked kitchen two water taps remained high and dry over an empty space where the sink had been wrenched out. The one thing that had not been plundered was the great black cooking range. It was a 'Daemon', cast in the city of Lille by the ironfounders *Dumont, Père et Fils*. I fiddled with the brass knob of its oven door.

'*Quelle est la solpe qui a montre ses fesses au rouquin?*' said the graffiti.

The Germans had captured the Moulin and smashed it.

'*Marie et moi on est montes une fois tirer un coup!*'

The French and the British had re-taken the Moulin and smashed it some more.

"Lens 3, Marseille 2. Vivent les Lensois."

Twenty years after the first World War had come the second.

Twenty years further on … a third World War was inconceivable wasn't it, in Europe, in 1965? We plunged back into the fresh air and picked our way through the Malbrancques' vine-tangled garden. Kenny lay on his belly to check the German machine gunners' angles of fire. An advantage of mere centimetres in elevation had given them command of heaven and earth.

"They couldn't have missed if they'd tried."

If the British guns had flattened the German wire, the Bareilly boys might have stood a chance. If the wind had been reliably from the west it might have blown the British gas straight to where it was intended and they might have stood a chance. But everything went wrong at the Battle of Loos and no one stood a chance It was another balls-up on a murderous scale. Kenny stood with a fixed look on his face. Inside the Malbrancques' long brick barn, great mounds of harvested beets glimmered like heaped skulls. The darkness smelled of organic fermentation.

"Kenny!"

From a thick beam, a boy was hanging by his neck on a length of orange baler twine.

"Have you never seen a scarecrow before?" said Kenny.

The boy's head was a carrier bag, his trousers were stuffed with straw. Scarecrow? I had not heard a crow all day, nor a single sparrow's cheep. No birds nested at the Moulin de Pietre. It was an evil place. Death lurked in every leaf and fibre. I stood with a hammering heart.

"Calm yourself," said Kenny, "for fucksake."

* * * * *

By 1000 hours on Saturday, 25th September, 1915, the Battle of Loos had reached its crisis. At the most northerly point of the ten-mile battle line, at Mauquissait, in front of the Moulin de Pietre, the Bareilly boys had reached their objective but were unable to take it. The decision that had to be made – to retreat, dig in, or to try again – rested with the Brigade commander, General Norie. He didn't have a clue. The phone lines had been cut by the German barrage. None of his runners had got through. Appeals for ammunition and reinforcements had not reached him.

"Basically," said Kenny, "we was fucked."

He had seen enough, more perhaps than he had bargained for. We re-crossed the Layes Brook but rather than return to the Pintoes the way we had come, through the cabbages and cauliflowers, Kenny chose a different route. Fifty yards from the Moulin he paused for the chance to look back.

"Funny about the birds," he mused. "A barn wi' no birds is something rare in this world."

We were stood in a great wide field sub-divided by drainage ditches, each filled with its seepage of groundwater. Kenny jumped the ditch in front of us and landed awkwardly and decided to give his ankle a rest. He hunkered down with his tin of makings. All around were drifts of dry, withered vines left over from the pea harvest. Kenny looked up suddenly, stiffened and sniffed the air.

"College," he said, "I think this might be it –"

His gaze stayed fixed on the Moulin and his full meaning became clear.

"Are you sure?" I said.

He cast about with a wary eye. We were sitting on a buried trench.

"Oh aye," he said. "It was here it happened, or hereabouts. Nothing's felt like this before."

The battlefield enclosed us. Here, on this ground, during the course of a single day, Kenny had faced a whole lifetime of fear. He handed me a shrapnel ball. It was about the same size and colour as a dried pea. No one who didn't know what he was looking for would have seen it.

"There was shrapnel everywhere that day," he said. "Like hail stones."

Fifty years on, the shrapnel still lay where Jerry had sown it. Kenny found another lead ball. I poked around and found one of my own. Once you knew what you were looking for, there was shrapnel everywhere. My head filled with the flame and smoke of battle. Was this was the place where Kenny and the squad had smoked their Turkish fags?

"The Turkish fags?" he said. "Christ, did I tell you that story? That wasn't here, son. That was in the Salient, 1917. Fucksake, we had no time for fags when we was hereabouts. It was life or death at the Battle o' Loos."

I supposed, disappointedly, that war stories were like that. You wore them out over time, mis-remembered them, got your facts mixed up – like me and my pomes.

"Jerry's second line was right here," he decided, "full o' dead and wounded. Blood and bits all over the place. Christ, it was a shambles. Sergeant Ross said we should stick to the plan and work our way to the flanks, but we were too late. Old Jerry had got his bombers there before us. And they had the range off pat. First thing we knew was when Sergeant Ross went round the next traverse and there was this bloody Hun corporal waiting for him. Christ knows how we got out o' there in one piece because three Jerry bombs came over, bang, bang, bang, but we got out somehow and started chucking our cricket balls back to ward 'em off."

Once the Germans in the Moulin realised they had stopped the Bareilly Brigade's charge, they counter-attacked, as per the doctrine of 1915. The Jocks, Leicesters and Gurkhas had pushed too far, too quickly. The Brigade's best men had been shot to pieces. General Norie knew none of it. He was keeping the Muzzie-boys of the 58th Vaughan's Rifles in reserve, to strike the decisive blow when opportunity beckoned.

"We needed more men," said Kenny. "We needed more bombs. We were chucking cricket balls as fast as we could prime the fucking things but only half o' them were going off because the fuses had all got damp. I was sitting there at the bottom o' the trench priming every one but they weren't going off when they was chucked. The fucking Jerries couldn't believe their luck. We had the range alright, but our fucking bombs were useless."

Cut off from support and facing a strong, revengeful enemy, Kenny's squad reached the same conclusion as everyone else. The game was over. The officers were all dead or wounded. No orders had come up from Brigade HQ. In the end, Colonel Walker decided to go back on his own to find out what to do. It was suicide, more or less. Colonel Walker had nothing to live for. His brave speeches, the hard work, the training and the marches, all had come to naught. The Fourth Black Watch had been sacrificed in a feint attack. The objective remained in enemy hands.

"We never saw him again," said Kenny.

The Germans moved their machine guns and snipers into shell holes. Their bombers infiltrated down the flanks. Sure of their superiority, they moved in for the kill.

"We were sitting ducks."

One by one, in scattered groups, the remnants of the Bareilly attack retreated, crawling from one bit of trench to the next. It was the same story along most of the Loos battlefront. The gas had gone awry. The bombs had been duds. The German wire remained intact. The distracting battle that Sir Douglas Haig had agreed to undertake on behalf of the French had turned into a blood-bath. Regiment after regiment had been reaped by the German machine guns – the Glaswegians of the Highland Light Infantry at Mad Point, the Seaforths at Fosse 8, the Argyll and Sutherland Highlanders at Cuinchy brick stacks. The Scottish battalions of the 15th Division did succeed in taking the coal-mining village of Loos, with Piper Laidlaw standing on the parapet to urge them on, but they went too far and lost direction and ended up like all the rest, in dead mounds. The Battle of Loos surpassed by far every previous slaughter of Scottish fighting men.

"You had to grab any bit o' cover you could find," said Kenny, "and stick to it. We still had a bucket o' them cricket balls left, and our rifles, so Sergeant Ross and Billy set up a bit o' covering fire for the rest o' us. Then Corporal Mackay fired his machine gun, over to the left. That was a case o' holy hallelujah when we heard that because it meant the two squads could cover each other."

With the Colonel gone and all the officers hit, Sergeant Ross's bombers and Corporal Mackay's machine gun contrived to take charge of their tiny sector of Hell. The wounded were dragged back by their less mangled comrades while the Germans bombed and sniped their way closer.

"They were like wolves, them Jerries," said Kenny. "They attacked and killed anyone that moved. The feelings that boiled up inside you —"

Kenny tested his weight on his twisted ankle and took a few wincing steps towards something he'd seen in the mud. It was the corner of a soldier's blue enamel water bottle. Kenny howked it out with his roguing stick and pulled away the rag of khaki cloth that wrapped it.

"Aha!" he murmured, turning it over in his hands. "This could have been mine. I lost everything that day, my bottle, my webbing. All I came out with was the boots on my feet."

"And your life," I said. "You came out with your life."

I reached into the quarter pocket of my jeans and pulled out the pen nib capsule containing the Punjabi scrip Kenny had given me a seeming age ago. He handed over his water bottle full of cold clay.

"So your Ma did help in the end?" he said.

Kenny ranged the translated scrip in front of his nose to find the focus and read aloud.

'But God shall rescue those who fear him into their safe retreat, no ill shall touch them, neither shall they be put to grief. Naik Ali Haidar. 58th V.R.'

Somewhere near us, Kenny had been saved and our Billy lost. The field was scattered with the dead and the dying. Wraiths loomed in the fog and disappeared.

"What does it mean, College?"

"It's a quote," I said. "From the Qu'ran, the Muslim holy book."

I had read every word in my father's book until I had found it. As for it's meaning, Kenny knew that better than I. On Judgement Day, when the gates of Hell opened and the earth cracked and the clouds rained fire, there was no hiding place for any man.

"*Naik* means corporal," I said. "You were saved by a corporal in the 58th Vaughan's Rifles. His name was Ali Haidar."

Kenny frowned at the translation and braced himself to face the vast, cathedral-like silence of the fog.

"We set up a trench block in Jerry's second line," he said, "but because it was a Jerry trench, everything was back to front. The firestep was the wrong way round. Sergeant Ross went out on top to see the lie o' the land. He was bleeding down his face because some cunt had shot his ear off. They'd hit our Billy too –"

Kenny stared into the mist. An obstruction had arisen.

"Have you a nip on you to spare?" I said. "It's a wee bit on the chilly side, this mist."

Kenny took a slug of his battle juice.

"They'd hit our Billy too," he said. "It looked like he had a squashed plum inside his top pocket. There was a stain there. He didn't seem to mind. He was out on top with the sergeant. I was down in the bottom o' the trench, crawling over dead boys to get their ammo. Pal Duncan just sat there, watching, with a look on his face I'd never seen before."

The first dram having hit the spot, Kenny followed up with a second and coughed some more.

"We called him Pal," he explained, "because that's what he called everyone else. 'How're you doing, pal?' "What's up, pal?' Pal this, Pal that, that was our Pally. And I was thinking to myself, 'Am I the only cunt's no been hit?' because suddenly I notice that Pally has just the one boot on. And I'm thinking to myself, 'What the fuck's going on? Has the whole world gone totally fucking bampot?' because our Pally was just sitting there with one boot on his one foot and a bandage on the other, trailing in the mud, all white and –"

Kenny turned his back and stabbed his roguing stick in the ground. One moment, Kenny Roberts had been down in the mud looking for ammo, the next –

"The next thing was," he said, "Sergeant Ross and Billy were sliding back down into the trench and telling us to get the fuck out because Jerry's bombers were coming straight over the top to get us. So we turned to leg it and who the fuck do you think we ran into round the next traverse – a squad o' your Muzzie-boys, that's who. They were hauling up a new load o' bombs for us."

"Muzzie-boys?"

"Four of your Vaughan's Rifles, I guess. Must have been. They were lugging up crates o' bombs with rope handles, one between two. By Christ, we were glad to see them. Our Pally took his bayonet to one o' the crates and had its lid off in a jiffy. Talk about the nick o' time. Old Jerry was almost on top o' us. We could hear him shouting – " 'Fuck you, Tommy. Fuck your sister. Fuck your mother.' "

Kenny's shoulders were shaking. He had started to laugh, silently, painfully.

"That really was the end," he said, "when we got inside them boxes o' bombs."

It was a calamity. It was hilarious. It was the worst joke ever.

"They were hairbrushes – French bombs we'd never seen before. And they weren't even assembled. The hairbrush came as a kit, see – a tin can with the explosive charge in it and a paddle o' wood for launching it. You were meant to clap the two bits together and fasten them before priming the fuse, which gave you five seconds to chuck the fucking thing. We'd only seen hairbrushes in training. And the instructions were all in Froggie lingo."

Rather than scrap their old-fashioned, unreliable hairbrush bombs the French had generously donated them to the British. The British, in turn, had generously passed them on to the boys of the Bareilly Brigade.

"Them Muzzie-boys just looked at us," said Kenny. "They couldn't believe the bombs they'd brought up were dud. One o' them held out the instructions to Sergeant Ross. It was no good. It was too late. Because we looked up and there was this bloody big Ger-boy with his bayonet, right on top o' us –"

Kenny had reached the end of his words.

"Hairbrushes," he said.

He re-lit his fag with a shaking hand.

"*Kaput*," he said. "*Fini la guerre.* A shell burst right on us, I guess."

One moment there was a squad, a trench, a box of useless grenades. The next moment –

"God knows how long I was knocked out for. I was deafened by it, that's for sure. All I could hear when I opened my eyes was this ringing in my ears. Our Billy was on his hands and knees wi' bits hanging off him. I shouted but I couldn't hear myself. I was completely deaf. But

Billy looked up at me and Jesus Christ his face was all blood."

Kenny uprooted his roguing stick and examined the quality of the mud at the end of it.

"And then?" I said.

"Another shell, I guess. Fuck knows."

One more big bang. Another Scottish blacksmith's son sent to oblivion. End of story. For fifty years Kenny had lived with his squad's wretched end.

"If I could have reached him, College –"

No one could have reached our Billy, or Sergeant Ross.

"It wasn't your fault."

Something rattled a nearby scutch of dried pea vine and a scared hare shot out like a brown streak, ears flat, black eyes bulging. Kenny knelt by the shallow basket of flattened vine stems that the hare's ribs had moulded in the earth. It was still warm.

"Read it me again College," he said softly. "I like the way you say them quotes."

I cleared my throat.

" 'But God shall rescue those who fear him into their safe retreat, no ill shall touch them, neither shall they be put to grief. Naik Ali Haidar. 58th V.R.'"

Kenny knelt awhile, head bowed, absorbing the heat of the hare's form through the palm of his hand.

"And amen to that," he said. "And have you by any chance got one o' them fancy French fags on you to share?"

"I thought you didn't like them."

"They're fucking shite," said Kenny. "But for some reason I want one."

I shook a Gauloise from its packet and handed it over. The strong, pungent smoke hung in the mist like a shape or portent. Kenny stirred it with his stick and watched it disperse. Slowly, grudgingly, we started walking again towards the Pintoes.

"Can you see what I see?"

The next field across the shallow ditch was full of potatoes. They had reached full maturity and collapsed in ripe exhaustion across their drills. Here and there, their hard green fruits peeped out like young tomatoes.

"Aha!" said Kenny. "And what kind o' variety do you think we might have here?"

They had thick dark stems and close-packed, hairy leaves. Perhaps, I suggested, the French had varieties of their own we knew nothing about. Perhaps it was a 'De Gaulle', or a 'Marie Antoinette'? I howked out a tuber with my heel and thumbed away the mud on it.

"It's not a Desiree," I said, indicating the pink skin. "It's too dark."

"It's a Champion I reckon," said Kenny. "I thought this variety had died out long ago. I haven't seen a Champ for donkey's years."

"Champion?"

"Named after the bloke who invented it," said Kenny. "William Worthington Champion. It was one o' the first crops Auld Andy tried when he started with the tatties before the last war. Big yield on it but the growers took against it. Terrible prone to blackleg was the Champion."

He bowled the tuber away with a stiff-armed bomber's heave.

"You do realise what we're doing?" I said. "We're roguing. On our holiday."

There was no proper endrig to the big field, only an empty strip for the tractors to turn in. We took our bearings on the Moulin for the last time. The black earth soaked up the grey mist. The conditions were perfect for potatoes. Flanders was very much like Fife in that respect. The field looked dull and empty unless you knew what you were looking for. Kenny coughed, cleared his throat and called his farewell.

"God bless you, Ali Haidar, wherever you are. And God bless Our Billy too. God bless you, boys. God bless."

The Fourth Battalion, the Black Watch, had gone into action against the Moulin de Pietre with 21 officers and 450 men. When the Quartermaster called the roll at the village of Pont du Hem at 1800 hours, Saturday, 25th September, 1915, one officer and 210 men answered their names. Kenny Roberts was crossed off as wounded. Billy Rankin was crossed off as missing. Kenny and I left that field of Champions and walked back to the Pintoes with nothing left to say.

17 THE HALLOWED

Kenny and I had planned to return the Pintoes to M. Bonneflage's garage after breakfast and head north by train to see if we could find Hill 60, the place near the Belgian town of Ypres where Kenny had been shot in the elbow in 1917. We did no such thing. We kept the Pintoes and after breakfast headed straight back to Mauquissait. The brooding solitude of the Moulin de Pietre held Kenny in thrall on account of the motorbike buried at Crean's ruined smiddy and the scar notched between Harry Blaine's eyebrows.

"It's no just me, College. It's the whole o' Murtry I'm remembering for."

We tramped the drills again and found the Layes Brook flowing as placidly as if it had never been dammed by Scottish and Gurkha corpses. We took our fag break at Salt Post, after Kenny ruled out Pepper because it smelled too much like a dried pond in which something had died unpleasantly. We smoked with our backs resting against bullet holes. The whole country had brightened with the change in the weather. Death had fled. Each leaf and fibre fizzed with Life.

"Fancy a nip o' my new French recipe?" said Kenny, passing it over. "I think you'll like it."

Rough cognac, barely diluted, brought tears to my eyes.

"Thanks for the warning," I spluttered.

The pigsties on the farm across the way were made from humped steel shelters disinterred from old British trenches. There wasn't much military hardware for which the French *paysan* hadn't been able to find a purpose after the war. About a quarter of the fence-posts around Mauquissait were iron piquets salvaged from the battlefield. Kenny breathed deeply on the reek of manure.

"Ah, that's beautiful that is."

Any landscape was beautiful to Kenny if it was being put to proper use.

"I still cannot believe it," he sighed, rising to his feet. "Fifty years ago, College, if we'd been standing here like this –"

First had come the Great War for Civilisation, then the cemetery makers, now the pilgrims. The sum of things worth saving had been saved, including the cultivation of root vegetables.

"If us two had been standing here fifty years ago," said Kenny, "we'd have been killed about a hundred times each by now. That's how thick the bullets were flying."

Two children rattled down the lane on bikes, cutting diagonally across No Man's Land from the German lines to the British. Winning the war had put Mauquissait back on the map. Peace had raised a new steeple on the church where once the sniper lurked. The war had been right because the Germans had been wrong.

"Aye," said Kenny, "war's a terrible thing but if enough blokes think they can get away with it, they'll try. Peace is just the bit between one war and the next, I reckon. There'll never be an end to war so long as some daft bastard thinks he can get away with it."

We finished our fags and walked to the Moulin de Pietre one more time, for old times' sake, and then kitted up at the Pintoes and headed back to Bethune. It didn't matter that we soon got lost. Whichever way we turned, sooner or later the pinnacle of the old belfry would appear to guide us. The British military cemetery at Le Touret took us by surprise with its grand arcade and Doric cloister.

"Now this," said Kenny, "this really is beautiful."

He shook off his gauntlets and caressed the stone. Here, surrounded by their Imperial symbols, slept the officers and men of the British Army *in perpetuam*. The Royal Artillery. The Grenadier Guards. Under each regimental crest was a roll of names, English and Scottish, carved in white stone, regiment by regiment in order of seniority. So many names. So many battalions. And not a Muzzie-boy among them. Always, wherever we went, I had found the same shaming lack of recognition of my boys.

Le Touret was a memorial to the Missing, those who had gone into battle never to be seen again. The nails in Kenny's boots rang out as he quickened his pace. In the middle of the cloister was a lawn. In the middle of the lawn was a plinth left eloquently empty.

"This is them," he croaked. "They're here."

The Missing of the Black Watch stood guard invisibly. Wise old Saint Andrew upheld his saltire. *Nemo me impune lacessit.* The regimental sphinx remained impassive.

Adamson, B ... Allan, M. C ...

Kenny slid his goggles up onto the peak of his helmet, leaving a goggle-shaped patch of cleanliness around each eye. He straightened the stoop in his shoulder. If he hadn't known it before, he knew now what had drawn him to France.

Anderson, W ...

Kenny stood before the wall of names and his eagle eye clouded over.

Black, P ... Black, G. M ...

 He had come to read these names.

Dillon, P. L. ... Duncan, B ...

Reading the names he remembered the faces.

"Pally," he gruffed, "it's me, old son."

Kenny set down his helmet and goggles and approached a step closer.

He read the names of the Black Watch and his squad answered.

Quin, P. ... Quinlan, C.W ...

Rae, J. B. ...

He raised his hand.

Rankin, W.

Kenny spelled out our Billy's name with his finger tips. Then he spelled out the name beneath it.

Ross, J. C.

The squad was together again. Duncan, Rankin, Roberts and Ross. The last man standing, Kenny Roberts, rested his forehead against the cool grain of the stone where his own name was not. His skinny old shoulders heaved under their Scottish tweed and something splashed onto the toe of his boot. It was so quiet I dared hardly breathe. Slowly, one backward step at a time, I withdrew to the Pintoes to stand sentry.

No one came. I signed the cemetery register. It seemed, from the dates, that Kenny and I were the first people to visit Le Touret in nearly six months.

'Scotland the Brave,' I wrote. '*Nemo me impune lacessit.*'

An old woman on the other side of the road was making a slow job of digging up her vegetable plot. A bonfire of damp leaves trailed smoke across the space between us. When she stopped for a rest she looked up and saw me and beckoned with urgent furtiveness.

"*Monsieur! Monsieur le Indien! Comment allez vous?*"

It was my paramour from the café. In a patch of gravel by her garden fence was a three legged chair with a tin box on it. A sign was written in a shaky hand.

'*Musée de l'Abris d'Emile Tardieu.* The Trench Museum.'

I slotted in a couple of francs and pushed through the gate. The old woman's unique aroma carried the full distance. It was her alright, as the wart on the chin confirmed. Her eyes glowed fervently.

"*Très interesant, Monsieur,*" she said. "*Très important. Vilcom. Vilcom. Regardez –*"

"Oi!" called a husky voice behind us. "What's going on? Are you trying to shake me off, young College, or what?"

Madame Tardieu paused in her twitter as Kenny caught up with us. Round to the side of the house, down some steps, was a Hobbit-like entrance to a low building that looked as if it had once been a commercial hot-house. The glass inside had been covered with thick, glaucous green paint.

"Sheesh!" said Kenny. "Look at this lot!"

The brick frames that had once grown lettuce and tomatoes now sprouted all manner of rusty trench weaponry, including a brace of mortars standing guard with black mouths agape. Grenades lay in neglected heaps. Madame picked up one of the notorious dud cricket balls.

"*Boum!*" she cackled, handing it over. "*Beaucoup des bombes pendant la Guerre.*"

"Christ, lad!" said Kenny. "Remember what I told you about them fuses. Tell her to take it easy or she'll blow us all to kingdom come."

The weapons of the trench war seemed medieval in their brutishness. Dented helmets lay in sorted piles, German, French and British. Kenny selected a Lee Enfield rifle and slid the bolt in and out while Madame watched approvingly. She handed him a rust-mottled bayonet.

"Wait till I see Fredo again," I said. "He won't believe I've seen you hoist an actual hype."

Kenny aimed at a tailor's dummy dressed in a German uniform. I picked up an officer's revolver and did likewise. Another of Madame's stiffly posed *tableaux* showed a French medic placing a cigarette between the lips of a prostrate German while a very realistic rat watched from under the stretcher. When I approached for a closer look, the rat scuttled off. At the far end of the room, covering the exit, was a canvas curtain. Behind it was the entrance to a trench, six foot deep, complete with damp-rotted revetments and duckboards. I mounted the fire step and peered through the loophole. It was the real thing. I was looking through an actual sniper's loophole with an actual bomber standing beside me.

"Well?" said Kenny. "What's Old Jerry up to today?"

I saw what a million teenage sentries had seen before me, rank grass and flat fields, all quiet on the Western Front. At the end of Madame's trench was an observation post with a slit at ground level camouflaged with branches. Inside, was a Vickers Mark One machine gun, a real one, a battered bit of kit that had been bashed about in battle. Kenny wriggled into the firing position.

"Ach! The front sight's missing. That's a great start. See what's in yon box, College."

I prised the lid off the lead-lined ammunition box and looked inside.

"Three dead snails," I reported.

"*Ici! Ici, Messieurs!*" insisted Madame, pulling at my sleeve.

Two stones, neither of them bigger than a football, had been set under the back fence. The old woman gestured.

"*Mes deux bebes musils.*"

The stones had been painted white. I didn't need a sign. *Musils* meant Muslims.

"Muzzie-boys?"

"*Deux,*" said Madame, holding up two fingers. "*Mes deux bebes musils.*"

She sank to her knees and pulled out a weed. The hairs rose on the back of my neck.

"Babies?"

Madame hauled herself up, touched my face and settled creakily at a garden table. From the open kitchen window came the sound of someone, Emile Tardieu presumably, rattling saucepans on the stove. A lame cat came out of the back door and lay at Madame's feet while another curled up in her lap. There was no seat for Kenny. He sat on his haunches with his back against the shed and his tin of makings on the ground in front of him.

Slowly, in dribs and drabs of Franglais, with my Lichfield French to help out, Madame Tardieu told me what had happened when ninety thousand Muslims, Sikhs and Hindus in British uniforms arrived in

French Flanders to drive back the Hun. She had never encountered such heady exoticism.

"She's right there," said Kenny. "I told you – your Muzzie-boys had to beat the womenfolk off with a stick they were so damned keen for it. They had no men o' their own, see. It was the same with us and the kilt. Christ, as soon as a *mamselle* saw the kilt she was there for the asking, *tray bon*. Same with the lads in the turbans, especially if they was on a horse."

In the Autumn of 1915, with Madame's two brothers at the war and their father trapped in Lille behind the German side of the Line, the womenfolk hereabouts had had to shift for themselves. Madame gave birth to a baby boy conceived of a Muslim soldier. Three weeks later her sister did the same. They tried to hide the consequences but one day Monsieur le Cure came to the door, having received a tip off. A policy had been approved in the war zone to allow women to deal with their illegitimate offspring without shame or recrimination; it was their patriotic duty to keep the gene pool untainted. At which point in Madame's story I felt the need to walk about the garden to compose myself.

"*Débarrasser?*" I said.

Disposed of. Expedited. Despatched.

'*Ils etaient si beau, si magnifiques, si courageux…*'

Madame's reservoir of tears for her half-caste babes had been cried out long ago. She bit her lip. The Muzzie-boys had crossed the black ocean to fight for a king they didn't know in a land that wasn't his and death had been their wage. These were their fields and this their sky. And their children had been disposed of.

"That's right," said Kenny. "She's right. The Froggies killed off their bastards if nobody wanted them. And nobody wanted the half-castes that's for sure, not in those days, not hereabouts."

The Battle of Loos had ended but the War continued. And I was in it, up to my neck in it. If Kenny had known about the bastards, everyone must have known about them. It was unbearable. Madame stroked her cat with sad eyes.

"How?" I asked. "*Madame? Comment ... les bebes?*"

She covered her eyes with her left hand and put the right one round her throat. Strangled. Smothered. Killed off like surplus kittens. It was unbearable.

"They kept the white ones," said Kenny, "or so I believe. If the white bastards were good looking they kept them, or gave them away to kin-less folk who could afford it."

My years of being English dragged me down.

"It was the war, son," said Kenny. "That's what I've been trying to tell you."

On my knees. I was down on my knees.

"It was a crime, Kenny. It was murder."

"No one's arguing with that, College. It certainly was a crime. But it was Jerry who did it. He committed the crime and it took a war to sort it out. The whole world was turned inside out in that war. Right and wrong went by the by on both sides. It was just war and more war until our lot won it."

* * * * *

The Fourth Battalion's first battle was its last. After distracting the

Germans at the Moulin de Pietre there weren't enough men left for
the regiment to be worth re-building. Dundee's finest, the Fourth
Black Watch, was struck off the roll of the British Army. Its survivors
were drafted into the Fifth Battalion to be used for mending roads.
As for the Muzzie-boys, having worn themselves out in the cause
of attrition they were shipped off to Mesopotamia to fight Johnny
Turk. The climate out there was deemed to be better suited to their
temperament. Kenny himself spent most of 1916 convalescing. His
maimed shoulder from the Battle of Loos kept him out of the Battle of
the Somme but he was re-trained as a machine gunner and sent back
to Flanders with a brand new squad in time for Passchendaele, 1917.

"Mebbe next year we can go back again?" said Kenny. "Mebbe we
could take a look at Eeps, the Salient. If I live that long. What do you
reckon? Will you and Fredo be back next year for the roguing?"

Kenny's train for Edinburgh hissed and steamed alongside
Platform 9. Overhead, the glass vault of King's Cross station buzzed
with the trapped echoes of departures and arrivals. He had claimed
his seat and stowed his bundle in the rack and was standing by the
carriage door rolling us a last cigarette, a thin one for me, a thinner
one for himself. My father's repaired and refurbished Corona told
me I had twenty minutes to get to Euston before my own train left for
Birmingham New Street and the connection to Lichfield.

"Aye," I said. "Mebbe we'll go back next year. Someone's got to get
you through the roguing now you're so weak in the knees and soft in
the head."

"You cheeky wee bastard."

The tempo of departure quickened around us. Whistles blew.

Kenny cleared his tubes and spat into the gap between train and platform.

"That was a good job o' work we just did," he said, nodding to the east. "Thank you, son."

He held out his calloused hand. The goodbye gland in my throat swelled instantly.

"Aye," I said, "we'll make a Muzzie-boy out o' you yet."

Kenny laughed and coughed and punched me on the upper arm and I punched him back.

"This is it then," he said. "*Au revoir, m'soo.*"

We avoided eye contact. Thank you, son. Aye. Take care of yourself. Aye.

"Fucksake, College," he said. "No need to look so miserable."

The porter strode towards us, slamming carriage doors. Kenny hopped aboard and stood at the open window.

"Fuck off, you too," I said, squinting against a tearful incursion of cigarette smoke.

"Aye," he said. "That's more like it. You just keep thinking up them inspirations o' yours, young College. Keep on quoting them quotes, you hear? That's what you're good at."

"And you give my love to Wilma," I said, "next time you see her. Which I'm sure you will before too long."

Kenny's eagle eye flared. Me and my inspirations, indeed.

"Wilma!" said Kenny. "Christ, what the fuck has Wilma got to do with anything? Eh? It's none o' your fucking business about me and Wilma."

The whistle blew again. The engine hooshed out steam and heaved on its couplings.

"I know what folk are saying about me and Wilma," shouted Kenny, "behind our backs. They can all go and fuck themselves."

"Relax," I shouted back, "your secret's safe with me."

I kept pace for a while as the train gathered speed. Kenny waved his cap. Then, as the guard's van cleared the end of the platform, the red lamp winked out and he was gone.

* * * * *

Kenny Roberts died on May 6th, 1966. The funeral took place on a bright, breezy Fife-ish morning at Crean kirk. Blossom filled the branches, the crops were showing nice and green all over the tillage. By the wall of the kirkyard lay a mound of fresh earth where a fox had scraped its earth. Rank grass tugged our ankles on the short walk to the grave.

After the interment, we mourners gathered at Lower Murtry big house where a subdued but dry-eyed Wilma had laid on a spread. The official cause of Kenny's death was lung cancer. Unofficially, we put it down to the delayed effects of Old Jerry's gas.

"Or mebbe," someone suggested, "he just got to the end."

We raised our drams and passed around the fags. It was going to happen to us all. A man worked his drill and sooner or later he came to the end of it. After that – well, no one really knew. After the drams and the fags and the ham sandwiches I took myself on a solitary walk up Crean Law and sat against the old boulders, absorbing whatever comfort they had to offer. I cried out my tears on the grass. I looked for Schiehallion but didn't see it.

The roguing at Murtry that year was pretty miserable, what with no Kenny around and poor old Shane moping about all day waiting for him to show up. Fredo and I stuck it to the end, partly for old times' sake, partly for the sake of Miss Jane and Big Lizzie, but there was no glory in the game without Kenny. It wasn't Bender's fault. We accepted him as gaffer, by virtue of seniority, but he would never be our leader. He hadn't fought the Jerry bastards to a standstill and lived to tell the tale. After a week with us Tamas left to join another squad for more money and we were all relieved. The work went easier after that but the old magic never returned and there was no ceilidh in the barn at the end of the season.

That was the last of our squad. The year after that, 1967, Fredo left St Andrews for Manchester and his clinical training. I heard that Tamas did eventually emigrate to Australia with the Princess of Gunnie but no reports that might have filtered home to Scotland ever found their way on to me. Bender went to Elmfield College to work for a diploma in mechanical engineering but dropped out after one term and ended up in the Fife constabulary, riding a motorbike. Wee Eck left Lower Murtry when his dad flitted to Dundee to drive the buses.

Eventually, after a lapse of years, I did go to Passchendaele in remembrance of Kenny; we stopped off there with the children one summer on our way to Provence. We stayed in Ypres and visited Hill 60 and some of the British war cemeteries of the Salient with me thinking of Murtry and the lads every step of the way. The next night we camped at Bethune to re-fight my part in the battle of Loos, 1915. When I knocked on the door at Madame Tardieu's cottage it was no longer a trench museum, I found a policeman living there.

He had got rid of the old glasshouse and filled in the trench and built a conservatory. I was kindly permitted access to his back garden but couldn't find the graves of the Muslim babies.

We did find Ali Haidar, however, or one just like him. His name was inscribed on a memorial to the Missing of the Indian Army at a place east of Bethune called Pont Logy. It was a fine monument in a modest kind of way, unostentatious and easily missable, which is how Kenny and I had both managed to miss it on our first pilgrimage. One *naik* called Ali Haidar was named at Pont Logy among the five thousand Muslims, Sikhs and Hindus who fought for the King-Emperor in Flanders but whose bodies were never found. It could have been him. I wanted it to be him, though I knew in my heart that the boys who'd been lost had been lost for ever, scattered to the wind. We can remember those we knew but the rest we can only mourn.

I often find myself wondering, when the wind is from the east, about the Battle of Loos, September 25th, 1915. Sometimes, sitting up here under the eaves, if the window is open to the night, I fancy I can still hear the guns on the Western Front, if the wind is from the right direction. I remember Kenny's hoarse oaths and his random pearls of wisdom. The photo postcard he gave me fifty years ago is staring straight back at me as I write these words.

"You keep it, son. That's what it's for, to remind folk after I'm dead."

18 WIND FROM THE EAST

The trusty Volvo noses its way through the streets of Finsbury Park and Kilburn with Rasgun lolling beside me, trussed into his seatbelt with his eyes closed and a drib of saliva on his chin. He is wearing the same clothes he went out in the night before. Slowly, London recedes into a smear of glum weather visible in the rear view mirror. The lorries in the slow lane of the M1 are moving faster than we are. We hit 70 m.p.h. for the first time just before Luton.

"Services ahead," says the navigator opening a gummed eye. "That's something to look forward to."

"Let's get some miles on the clock," I reply, "before we start thinking about Services."

The M1's succession of white on blue signs invoke the legendary destinations of my youth, Hemel Hempstead. Whipsnade Zoo. The North. Rasgun thinks he knows all there is to know about road trips thanks to his gap year holiday in America with two of his school pals. His last postcard is still pinned to the cork board in our kitchen: 'Dear Old Folks, Albuquerque sucks. Luv, Raz xxx.'

"I need calories," he groans. "I need caffeine."

"You should have eaten your breakfast. There's plenty of calories in two Weetabix and a spoonful of sugar."

When I was Rasgun's age there was no such adventure as a gap year, the M1 itself was considered excitement enough. Every Christmas, as a special treat, Grandad would take us down to London at 65 m.p.h. to see the Oxford Street lights, stopping on the way for a jam doughnut at Watford Gap Services.

"If I don't get coffee soon," says Rasgun, "I will die. And it will be your fault. And mum will never forgive you."

My grandad used to wear gloves for motorway driving. They were made of pig's hide and knitted string. At the first sign of car-sickness it was my mum's job to distract me with a game of I-Spy.

"I spy with my little eye something beginning with … A!"

"Asshole," says Rasgun. "Can't you see – *I'm too hungry to spy.*"

'A' was for apple when I was a boy. Grandad kept one on standby in the Rover's glove compartment alongside his AA Members' Handbook and the album for Green Shield stamps.

"If you're so hungry," I say, "help yourself to the apple."

"I don't like apples."

Once upon a time, a car's glove compartment was where its driver kept his driving gloves and the fast lane of the motorway was for going fast in. Apples were good for you when I was nineteen years old. Rasgun spurns anything that's good for him as a matter of principle.

* * * * *

Cropley Wood Services was not part of the plan when the M1 was first built, it's a Twenty-First Century addition. Under a great glass ziggurat proletarians throng the food mall in their team colours, clouding the air with glottalised, football-obsessed babble.

"Relax," says Rasgun. "It's a pit-stop. They're only people."

Since the latest bombings, Britain's public spaces have become contested ground for people like me. Rasgun fits in perfectly. No savvy chav is going to come up to him and say, 'Oi, Mustafa! Where's your turban?'

"For God's sake! Chill, will you."

I follow my nose to the organic pizzas while Rasgun opts for a double cheeseburger with fries. We find each other, bearing plastic trays, at a vacant, un-wiped table next to a woman with a spider tattoo on her neck. She fiddles with an unlit cigarette while stealing her kids' chips.

"They should be at school shouldn't they? It's not half term."

"Behave yourself," glares Rasgun. "Here, read something. You like reading."

He hands me the cartooned paper liner from his burger tray.

'All our burgers are made from 100% beef – no additives, no fillers. Our fresh dairy ice cream is exactly that – fresh every day. Our irresistible fries are made only from the choicest potato varieties – Russet Burbank, Shepody and Pentland Dell.'

"Russet Burbank?"

In an imaginary agri-lab I see whitecoated geneticists bending the veggie DNA into new potato shapes while next door, in Marketing, lively young folk dream up marketable names for them. What on earth is a Shepody? The names of a hundred potato varieties have vanished in my lifetime. What was wrong with Queen Mary, Arran and The Provost?

Rasgun takes the change from his burger to the games arcade. He's got a cricketer's eye, alright. With a laser gun in his hand he's as cool as a trained killer. I watch with baffled pride as he massacres robopunks, splattering the screen with their wired corpses. When the 'game over' siren sounds he gets a refund and puts the money straight back in.

"Stretch your legs," he says. "I might be a while."

A bridge of steel and glass connects Cropley Wood's mini-Babylon with its twin ziggurat on the other side of the motorway. I watch the traffic unspool beneath my feet, bumper to bumper, north to south and back again. Too many cars, not enough road, that is the problem. Too many white vans whizzing absentee fathers and their power tools to speculative building jobs too far from home. It is not quite the England I was expecting to inherit when I was Rasgun's age.

* * * * *

At Junction 18, the Volvo leaves the M1 and heads up the Watling Street into the heartland, the geographical dead centre. When I was a boy, Junction 18 was the precise point where holiday adventures began and happy home-comings ended. A hypermarket now occupies the site of the lay-by where the AA patrol man used to lurk with his motorcycle and side-car. I adored receiving his smart salute and giving it back.

"Is this going to take long?" says Rasgun. "This trip down Memory Lane?"

Angliae cor, the heart of Roman England. Grey clouds press down on all that's been lost.

"This is your heritage, Raz. You want to study History don't you?"

The factory chimneys I knew by name – 'Smith-Cozens', 'Browning Bros Fittings' – have been toppled and carted away. Roundabouts and one-way traffic systems have squashed flat the Anglo-Saxon's furrowed fields. The Volvo comes to rest in The Avenue and we listen to its engine ticking as it cools. Rasgun frowns at house where I used to live when I was his age. Speculative builders have joined the two semi-detached houses internally and added a fire escape at the back. A pseudo-Victorian conservatory has replaced the wooden garage where the trusty Rover slept night after night, dripping oil into its tray of sand.

'The Firs. Residential Nursing Home. Registered and Approved.'

The tops of the Scots pines loom over the back garden where Grandad used to help with my cricket. He wasn't permanently grumpy, just a man of few words – though he was voluble enough, by all reports, when my mother came home in mourning in January 1946, husband-less, with me in her arms, swaddled against my first English winter. Grandad did not stint himself then, nor on several subsequent occasions, when it came to venting his feelings on the subject of pre-marital miscegenation and its consequences.

"Mutability, Rasgun. Nothing stays the same."

Gone is the cube of opaque glass that used to hang over The Firs' front porch with the potent word SURGERY painted on it. Grandad used to switch on that lamp on his way to bed and off again when he came down each morning. After he died my mother took over and when she died the flame went out for good.

"Mutability," says Rasgun. "I'll try to remember."

On just such a day, Grandad, my mother and I climbed into the Rover and headed off in choked silence to New Street Station, Birmingham, leaving an empty nest behind.

"It was steam trains in those days. The whistle blew and off I went, chuff-chuff ..."

"Ace anecdote. Got any more like that?"

Families with sarcastic teenagers don't live in The Avenue any more. Most of the bigger houses have been divided into flats for singletons. Nor is The Firs the only nursing home. Caring seems to be one of Lichfield's few remaining industries.

"Perhaps we can dump you and Grandma here," says Rasgun kindly, "when we can't stand the smell of your pee any longer. You could play chuff-chuffs on your hands and knees and rail against the downfall of civilisation. You'd like that."

I fire up the Volvo and head back towards the one-way system. Somehow, we end up at my old school. The Library has been excitingly re-launched as a Learning Resource Centre and everything looks smaller than I remember. Across the fissured playground I spy the window of what used to be my old History class. In there, in keeping with the pioneering, inter-disciplinary trend of the Sixties, Mr Cramp used to quote from Wilfred Owen and Siegfried Sassoon to illuminate what our 'Modern Times' textbook had to say about the First World War.

"School's crap," says Rasgun. "Let's get out of here."

Out on the playing field, the cricket square seems sadly diminished. For decades I have cherished the memory of that glorious day when I hit 20 runs in one over off the school's best bowler and everyone decided to stop calling me a wog, at least to my face. I became Dolly after that – after Basil D'Oliveira, whose pigmentation stopped him being picked to play cricket for South Africa. When Dolly changed sides and took an English passport and came to play for Worcestershire it made people like me worthy of respect. He was my hero until Bob

Dylan came along. Then I had two heroes.

"He was a great player, Dolly. Elegant. Brave. You couldn't keep your eyes off him."

Rasgun hates school because of Maths and Physics not because he gets tripped up in the corridors from behind because he's a black bastard. I pull him close in the cricketer's hug.

"Let go," he says, "you soppy old twit."

One day Rasgun will understand me better. When he has a grandson of his own perhaps.

* * * * *

Edinburgh welcomes careful drivers with a cool wind all the way from Siberia. Rasgun shivers by the Volvo's open door, gazing up at the blue sky. We are numb in body and spirit from all the motorway miles we've left behind us. On a high column in the middle of the square a toga-clad old duke turns his cold shoulder.

"Why didn't you tell me it was going to be like this?"

This is Scotland, Raz. This is what it's like in the cricket season."

He goes to the back of the car to get his coat while I fiddle around with the parking ticket machine. Then we head off looking for a quick place to eat with the collar of Rasgun's leather jacket turned up.

"Your mum stole that jacket from me when she went to university."

"Well it's mine now," he says. "I found it in the shed. Come on, I'll buy you a pint and a pie if you lend me the money."

Afterwards, restored in body and soul, the Forth Bridge bears us smoothly over the redundant jetties where English armies and Scottish royalty once waited for the ferry. Rasgun cares nothing for the romance of long ago, he just wants to arrive.

'Welcome to the Kingdom of Fife. Please drive safely.'

Rasgun sends and receives text messages, switches on the radio and turns it off. It is too late in the day for another game of I-Spy. With the end now in sight, our little road movie is turning into a straightforward A to B delivery job.

"I'm so fricking bored," he says. "How much further is it to Dunkeld? I want to see the pitch while it's still light."

"Bored?" I reply. "How can you be bored? This is Fife, lad, the kingdom. What else do you think I've been talking about?"

The big house we're heading for at Dunkeld turns out to be a castle at the end of a glen. Rhododendrons flame purple, red and orange along the narrow road. Rasgun texts ahead to signal our imminent arrival. It feels like driving into the glossy pages of an upper-caste estate agent's brochure. I nose the Volvo into a space between a gleaming Maserati and a Mercedes.

"Who is this Nigel friend of yours? Some kind of lord's son?" Rasgun slips his phone into his pocket.

"He's a banker. Nigel's dad owns a bank. That's where the money is, Grandad."

Trance music wafts over from the marquee rigged up for tomorrow's cricket match.

"I'm glad you've made some friends at that school of yours. Even if they are all skunkaholics."

Watched by Victorian gargoyles we amble down to inspect the pitch. A couple of yellow labradors bounce up, followed by Nigel and his friends, boys and girls, a grown up or two, younger siblings, more dogs. Fairy lights glimmer. The pitch is in prime condition and the batsmen take courage. When Rasgun goes inside with his mates to dump his kit the lord and lady of the house press me to stay but I don't fancy being the token ethnic at the feast; I've got my own plans. I shake hands all round, settle the pick-up details with Rasgun and make my excuses. An hour later I drive into St. Andrews with the sunset unfurled behind me like a blazing banner.

"Shit a brick!"

The cobbled end of Market Street has been transformed into a garish souk of cappuccino outlets. What happened to all those shoemenders, locksmiths and 'dry goods' merchants? I settle the Volvo for the night and wander off to find a Bed & Breakfast. A smelly dog lies across the threshold of the television lounge, where the chatelaine has been catching up with the weather forecast.

"There's a chill in the air tonight," she announces, brushing crumbs from her bosom.

Her mood changes when she sees who she's dealing with. It's the same whenever there's been a bit of bombing on the news. My fellow citizens never think of Basil D'Oliveira nowadays when they meet me for the first time. Thank you, Osama bin Laden.

"A double room for just the one night is it?" Every stranger is a risk these days.

"Breakfast is seven-thirty to nine-thirty. The front door's locked at midnight."

My room smells of a chronic absence of ventilation. A weld on the radiator's control knob ensures that the heating level can never be set higher than 'LOW'. The coverlet on my bed is constructed of a harsh, flame-retardant material designed to be inhospitable to human contact.

I'm back, lads! The saft, wally English bastard is back!

I open the window and shut it again. Beyond the ruined pile of Castle Rock the North Sea's grey waves roll in. Two windsurfers tumble in the foam taking advantage of the last of the daylight. In my young day they'd have been arrested as a public nuisance.

* * * * *

I wake up with the sun in my eyes, befuddled by the lack of oxygen in the room. On the bedside table is the novel that put me to sleep last night. Next to it glows a text message on my phone regarding an urgent change of plan up at Dunkeld.

'Can u pick me up now please?'

It's that uncharacteristic 'please' that makes it urgent. I gobble down some toast and pay for the bed. The Volvo finds Rasgun squatting by the baronial gates, smoking a fag with a glum look on his face.

"What on earth's happened?"

"Nothing's happened. Calm down."

"So why are you leaving? You're letting the side down. They'll be a man short."

Rasgun throws his kit bag in the back and climbs in the passenger seat.

"Why does everything have to mean something to you?"

"You can't leave your squad in the lurch!"

"I left them a note."

"You don't say goodbye with a note. That's bad manners. You won't get another invitation."

"Good," says Rasgun. "I don't want another invitation. They can stick it up their arseholes."

He plugs in his earphones and silence prevails until the motorway powers us over the border from Perthshire into Fife, at which point I start looking out for any farms or fields I might recognise. When I point out the old barn at the Frasers' place where Fredo wooed Miss Jane all Rasgun sees is a messed-up old barn.

"I really need some breakfast," he says.

"You're too late. Breakfast around here is strictly from seven-thirty to nine-thirty a.m."

"In which case, what about lunch? You must be starving too." Nothing could be duller, on Rasgun's empty stomach, than my blethers about tatties and the squad and Miss Jane.

'Old Park Country House Hotel & Leisure Spa,' says the sign. 'Full Carvery menu. Non-residents welcome.'

A private road of red tarmac carves into the side of the hill like a sabre slash. The old park has been laid out as a golf course. Deer nibble daintily in the rough.

'Speed bumps. Strictly 10 mph.'

The innards of the old farm steading, dated 1888, have been scooped out to accommodate a glass-walled swimming pool. Two dripping children stand inside drawing faces in the condensation with the tips of their fingers.

"The last time I was here," I announce, "there was no roof on the place."

A kneeling Aphrodite maintains the water level of the dredged lake from an ever-flowing amphora. In a southward facing alcove, perfectly proportioned for a sundial, stands a broken memorial column. The new management, to its credit, is treating the ancestors of Dunbog House with respect. It welcomes me back with an unblinking stare from a surveillance camera. In the restaurant, as soon as Rasgun places his mobile phone on the table, it rings.

"I'll have the roast beef please," he says, heading back outside with the phone to his ear. "With all the trimmings."

From the window near our table I see my grandson pacing up and down, gesticulating for emphasis as he explains himself to those he has left in the lurch. A groundsman in Old Park livery is also out there, tending the sunny sand traps round the eighteenth green. Inside, a dynasty of fake ancestors gazes down from gilded frames. The Fyvies have fled, the ghost in the mirror is me.

* * * * *

A raw scar disfigures the worn face of Crean Post Office where its red 'V.R.' collection box has been wrenched out and bricked-in with minimal concern for cosmetic appearance. Speculative builders have also been at work on the old school, replacing its windows with double glazed units. Satellite dishes sprout like fungi. When the Volvo halts at the halt sign at the crossroads, Rasgun jolts awake in his seat belt.

"Is this it?"

The turning to Pittendrie Top opens on the left, then Wauchope's farm gate on the right. Down the brae we coast, through the tunnel of oak trees, past the keeper's lodge of the Dalbeattie estate towards the distant chimneys on the Lower Murtry big house.

"I don't believe it!"

The Wank Hut has vanished.

"The what hut?"

At the bottom of the hill I stop the Volvo by the culvert that once led to the track that once led to the old bothy where Fredo and I once lived fifty years ago. No track. No bothy. The Morrisons' fields of berries and potatoes have gone. The home fields of Wester Murtry and Lower Murtry have been merged into one long mile of fence-less arable.

"Grandad, did I hear you right? You and Fredo lived in a *wank* hut?"

No hedges, no gates, no need. No one in north Fife keeps cattle or sheep any more. Forget the old ways. Centuries of pasture and tillage have been rolled flat under a carpet of barley.

"A hut," says Rasgun, "for wanking in?"

"It's gone."

"*Shame!*"

The Volvo rolls us gently down the last of the incline towards the turning into the Lower Murtry yard.

"The old steading's gone too."

Dark clouds are piling up over the Sidlaw Hills. Rasgun turns up his leather collar while I shrug myself into the spare anorak covered in Rufi's dog hairs. The new barn that Davy Morrison built looks smaller than my memory of it. The end of one gutter hangs in midair, ready to pour rainwater into the yard the next time it rains, which could be any moment now.

"So," says Rasgun, inhaling on his Marlboro Lite. "This is it, the place you wanted to see so much?"

My memories don't fit. The windows of the cottage where Wee Eck used to live with his mum and dad are curtained with grime. No one gives a damn any more. The shed that held Wee Eck's collection of birds' nests has gone.

"All is mutability," observes Rasgun helpfully.

Wilma's bee hives lie in rotted heaps along the orchard wall behind the big house. No roses frame the kitchen door, nor does Wilma come bustling out with a basket of clean laundry on her hip. Oh Wilma, my Wilma! Three giant grain silos buzz ominously on the exposed concrete foundation of what used to be Wee Eck's dad's milking parlour. A big sign says it all: 'Lower Murtry Farm. Alexander Gillanders & Sons. Grain Merchants.'

We turn our backs on the desecration wrought by 21st Century agri-business and head up towards Crean Law the back way on foot, pausing in the wood to inspect the contents of the old quarry.

"There was a fox used to live around here, Raz – a notorious poultry stealer. If we ever saw him we were under orders to throw stones at him."

"You cruel bastards."

The sump of black water in the quarry bottom used to be where the men of Lower Murtry tipped their unwanted chunks of brickwork, split planks and redundant gates.

"That fox got into Queenie Morrison's precious flock of black hens one night and tore their heads off. There was a price on its head after that – a florin."

Murtry quarry's modern dumpings include the kind of stuff no one would have dreamed of discarding in 1965 – bikes, fridges, microwave ovens. I catch the scent of wild garlic. Two white scuts disappear into the undergrowth. No fox lives hereabouts these days, the old line's extinct. At the top of the hill we tarry a while to rest against the old boulders, sitting in silence except for the crows.

"They called me an octoroon," says Rasgun.

"Who did?"

"Nigel's sisters. When I looked over their shoulders to check the team sheet I saw they had given us all nicknames and mine was 'the octoroon.'"

"That's probably my fault," I say. "You shouldn't have turned up with your woggie grandad as your chauffeur. That probably reminded them."

"I said: 'Why have you named me after a cake?' I Googled it later. The bitches."

"They're not bitches. They were just being themselves. And anyway, according to some dictionaries, you are an octoroon. I'm a half-caste and your mother has a touch of the tar brush – that makes you an octoroon."

"I'm as English as they are."

I point with my partially chewed grass stem.

"Sitting here like this," I say, "I'm actually feeling a wee bit Scottish. See down there, round the corner? When I last sat here there was a ruined bridge down there, a pile of stones that showed where the old road used to be. The Wallace was reputed to have fought off a party of English skirmishers at that bridge, when he was on the run, centuries ago."

Genes propel us into the world, then people take over, and forces beyond our control,the big stuff that's hard to understand.

"If Nigel's sisters want to embarrass themselves at cricket matches," I suggest, "let them. It's not your problem."

"But what should I have said?" says Rasgun.

"You didn't have to say anything. People can only be themselves. The rest of us have to get on with it."

Each man has his drill to rogue and, if he's lucky, companions beside him. And when you get to the end of your drill, that's it. The life Raz is living right now is the one he will have lived when the end comes in sight.

"Come on, then," he sighs, brushing down the back of his breeks, "might as well get on with it."

I sit for an extra moment, willing Schiehallion to send me a message. Those whom I seek remain missing, gone but not forgotten. I remember the men I knew who loved Fife more than themselves. I remember those I never met who crossed the dark waters a hundred years ago to pass through fire. I pull myself up on the offered hand, dust down the seat of my breeks and follow Rasgun downhill the way we came, carefully, one step at a time.